"I think Cinderella is perfect for you," Master Wu said. "It's the English equivalent of your Chinese name, Ye Xian!"

"Yes!" Big Aunt agreed. "*Chinese* Cinderella—but that's such a mouthful. Why don't we just use the initials and call you CC?"

And that is how I got my English name, CC.

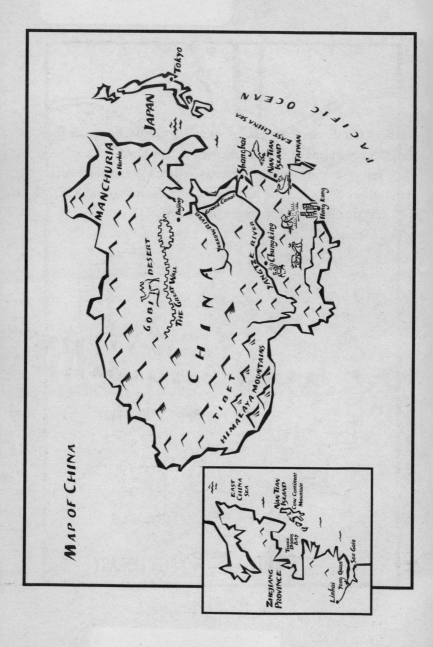

MAP OF CHINA

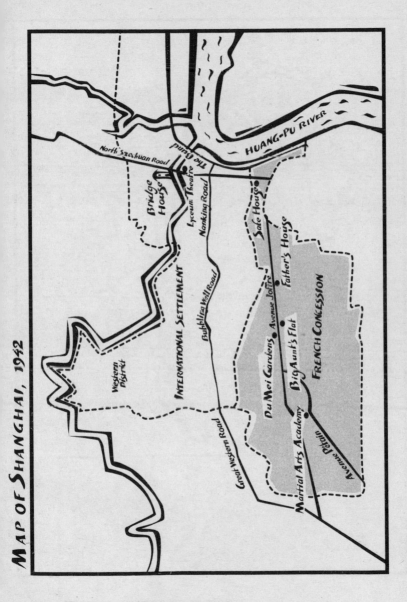

MAP OF SHANGHAI, 1942

HUANG-PU RIVER

North Szechuan Road

The Bund

Bridge House

Lyceum Theatre

Nanking Road

Safe House

Father's House

INTERNATIONAL SETTLEMENT

Bubbling Well Road

Avenue Joffre

FRENCH CONCESSION

Western District

Du Mei Gardens

Big Aunt's Flat

Great Western Road

Martial Arts Academy

Avenue Pétain

CHINESE CINDERELLA
and the
SECRET DRAGON SOCIETY

Adeline Yen Mah

■ HarperTrophy®
An Imprint of HarperCollins*Publishers*

ACKNOWLEDGMENT

A big thank-you to Ike Williams and Erica Wagner for their belief and inspiration. I also wish to acknowledge my U.S. editor Phoebe Yeh and assistant editor Whitney Manger for their able assistance and hard work.

HarperTrophy® is a registered trademark of
HarperCollins Publishers.

Chinese Cinderella and the Secret Dragon Society
Copyright © 2005 by Adeline Yen Mah
Interior illustrations by Fred van Deelan

Library of Congress Cataloging-in-Publication Data
Mah, Adeline Yen.
  Chinese Cinderella and the Secret Dragon Society / Adeline Yen
May.— 1st ed.
    p.   cm.
  Summmary: After her father and stepmother throw her out of their house
in Shanghai, China, twelve-year-old Ye Xian is taken in by a martial arts
group, the Dragon Society of Wandering Knights, and joins them and her
aunt in a mission to help the Americans fight the Japanese. Includes histor-
ical notes.
  ISBN-10: 0-06-056736-8 (pbk.) — ISBN-13: 978-0-06-056736-1 (pbk.)
  1. China—History—1937–1945—Juvenile fiction. [1. China—
History—1937–1945—Fiction. 2. World War, 1939–1945—China—
Fiction. 3. Martial arts—Fiction. 4. Spies—Fiction. 5. Aunts—
Fiction.] I. Title.
PZ7.M27633Ch 2005   2004008852
[Fic]—dc22

Typography by Larissa Lawrynenko
❖
First Harper Trophy edition, 2006

This book is dedicated to my childhood friend Wu Chun-mei and to all the children who enjoyed reading *Chinese Cinderella*, especially those who are unloved and unwanted and who have nobody to turn to.

I feel a great sense of responsibility toward those children who wrote to me after reading my books. Adults and children read for different reasons and in different ways. Adults read for entertainment and relaxation. Children read in order to learn about life. I remember very well the books I read as a child and their effect on me. Nothing in my adult life could equal the thrill and excitement I felt while reading *The Little Princess* when I was ten. It is estimated that children (on an average) read only about five hundred books before the age of twelve. However, as a child grows into adulthood and old age, no other books will affect her so deeply again. I wish to thank those children who have written to tell me that reading *Chinese Cinderella* has changed their lives. You have no idea how much that means to me!

CONTENTS

AUTHOR'S NOTE

During my lonely childhood in Shanghai, books were my only companions. I remember vividly the first book my aunt Baba read to me when I was three years old. It was colorful and loosely bound like a stack of flash cards. Each detachable page had a picture of an animal on the front and the appropriate Chinese character on the back. This book was special because my aunt had bought it just for me. Even after more than half a century, I can still hear the timbre of her voice, see the lifelike, detailed drawings and feel the warmth and comfort of her lap as she introduced me to the world of the written word.

Later, at primary school in Shanghai during the 1940s, Aunt Baba subscribed to a portable library run by an elderly, scholarly-looking bookseller. His movable stall was in a public park that I visited on my way to and from school. Tattered paperback *kung fu* novels were displayed on wooden racks resembling window shutters. For fifty cents, paid in advance by Aunt Baba, I could borrow five books per week.

The characters in these novels became more real to me than my family at home. They inspired me to write *kung fu* novels of my own, incorporating stories from my teachers and classmates, especially my best friend, Wu Chun-mei, who liked nothing better than going to the movies. Although I could never accept her invitations, she always entertained me with summaries of the films she had seen.

One of the movies she related from beginning to end was *Thirty Seconds Over Tokyo*, starring Spencer Tracy and Van Johnson. It was based on a true incident during World War II. Japan had invaded China and occupied many Chinese provinces along the coast. On December 7, 1941, Japan bombed Pearl Harbor in Honolulu. In retaliation, American planes carried out a bombing raid on four Japanese cities four months later. The U.S. pilots flew on to China after the raid, planning to land in an area controlled by Chinese troops. Unfortunately, they ran out of fuel, and some planes were forced to crash-land in Japanese-occupied territory. A few airmen were caught, but the majority escaped into western China with the help of the local Chinese people.

I spent an entire weekend writing a novella based on that movie and titled it "The Ruptured Duck." I remember getting up at dawn on Sunday morning in the dark in order to finish. I held a flashlight in my left hand while writing with my right so as not to disturb my aunt, who was still sleeping. When I finally scribbled, "The End," seventeen hours later that evening, I was filled with a tremendous sense of accomplishment and euphoria. I told my aunt that I'd rather write than do anything else.

"Why do you like it so much?" Aunt Baba asked.

"Because I'm free to say anything I wish, and nobody can stop me. More than that, I write because I must! It drives away everything that makes me sad. I can invent my own world and make it a beautiful place."

Back at school I showed "The Ruptured Duck" to Wu Chun-mei. She insisted on sharing it with everyone else. It thrilled me to see my writing being fought over by my class-mates. My manuscript was passed from desk to desk until our teacher confiscated it.

After the publication of my first children's book, *Chinese Cinderella*, I received many letters from young readers asking for *kung fu* stories similar to the ones I used to write as a child. So here is the first one.

This book is modeled on "The Ruptured Duck." To my sur-prise, many of the feelings I had as a child writer came back as I sat in front of my computer. My imagination transported me back to the same magical land I used to roam as a ten-year-old. In that place, the rules were always fair and everything was possible.

Let me emphasize that the heroine CC is a fictional char-acter whom I invented. Although there are similarities, this book is not an autobiography, and CC is not me. CC never existed in real life. Unlike my mother, CC's mother did not die in childbirth. CC was an only child, whereas I had four brothers and two sisters. CC's aunt lived separately in her own apart-ment. CC was a secret agent who was being trained in *kung fu*. I never had that privilege.

Let's roll the clock back across the time zones and pretend that you are Wu Chun-mei and I'm Yen Jun-ling. You and I are classmates and best friends at Sheng Xin Primary School in Shanghai. I'm handing you this book and saying to you, "I wrote this story over the weekend and finished it on Sunday so you can read it today. It was inspired by the movie *Thirty Seconds Over Tokyo*, which you told me about last week. I hope you'll like it."

CHAPTER 1

The Boy Acrobats

T WAS A SUNNY AFTERNOON in early spring when I set off after school to Big Aunt's place for my daily English lesson. I was thinking of a *kung fu* novel I was reading about a warrior monk with an iron hand as I hopped off the tram near the Du Mei Gardens, opposite my aunt's apartment.

The sounds of a bamboo flute drifted on the air with the heady fragrance of lilac blossoms, and suddenly I saw three boys, wearing colorful satin costumes with matching caps of red, blue and green, rounding a rhododendron bush into the park. I knew Big Aunt would worry if I was late, but I couldn't resist following them.

A large crowd was milling around the music pavilion, and an elderly woman signaled to the boys to hurry. Soon they were twisting, jumping and performing somersaults, all under the direction of the woman. The crowd gasped as one of the boys threw a bright red apple high into the air while his companion shot a dart from a sling and pierced it. I squeezed through the crowd. The boys were so lithe, strong and graceful; I couldn't take my eyes off them as they leapt and danced and caught each other, their wavy dark hair flopping into their faces.

One of the taller boys lay down on a wooden bench. I could see his chest rising and falling as he caught his breath. The shortest boy balanced a series of stools on his outstretched feet, one by one, higher and higher. Finally, the flute player climbed onto the highest stool. Nonchalantly, he began to play a tune I recognized as one that my father used to sing when he was in a good mood. As the music reached a crescendo, the boy lying down suddenly kicked his heavy load up into the air. Deftly, the woman caught the falling stools while the flute player somersaulted back to the stage. He grinned and started to play a new tune.

The crowd burst into applause, and I couldn't help clapping too. The smallest boy now appeared on a unicycle, darting around the stage set up in front of the pavilion as his companions tied a thick rope between two high platforms. When the rope was taut, the boy carried his unicycle to the top of a platform and balanced it carefully. I held my breath. Now he was riding his unicycle across the rope suspended high above the ground, bobbing his head in time to the music. The flute player followed, playing his instrument, and then the tall boy sprang onto the rope, juggling colored balls as he went. When the unicyclist climbed down from the platform, he nodded at me and winked before putting on his glasses. I blushed because I knew he had seen me watching him with my mouth open!

The show continued with magic tricks—the boys making cards and coins disappear and then pulling them out of hats, shirts and pockets. They laughed and joked while the audience cheered and clapped. Then the flute player approached the audience with his cap, asking for contributions. When he came to me, I was embarrassed. I looked down at my feet and muttered that I had no money.

"Did you enjoy the performance?" he asked, smiling.

"Yes. Very, very much! This is the best show I've ever seen!" I didn't tell him that it was the *only* show I'd ever watched in my life.

"Did you say that you have no money?"

"That's right. Not a single cent! I wish I had some to give you. Your show was great!"

"But you *do* have money!" he said. Then he pulled a coin out of my right ear, held it to the light, inspected it and dropped it into his hat. As the audience clapped, he pulled something else out of my other ear and held it to the sun. It was a business card.

"Hello! Hello! What have we here?" he exclaimed as he waved the card in the air and pretended to examine it. "All sorts of hidden treasures are coming out of your head via your ears! Your mother must have forgotten to wash them this morning!" He smiled and handed me the card. The audience roared.

"Keep it!" he said. "One never knows. You might need our help one day." Then he moved on.

I looked at the card, which read:

LONG XIA HUI　龍俠會

DRAGON SOCIETY OF WANDERING KNIGHTS
Martial Arts Academy
Plaza in Du Mei Gardens &
2200 Avenue Pétain, Shanghai

We help the oppressed and downtrodden.
We show the *tao*—way—to those who are lost.
Martial Arts. Judo. Karate. Boxing. Kickboxing. Acrobatics.
Chinese Classics. Poetry. Calligraphy. Brush Painting. Music.

I read the card over and over and put it in the pocket of my school uniform. What did it mean, Dragon Society of Wandering Knights? Who were these people? I crossed the road to Big Aunt's apartment, fingering the card and wondering what it would be like to be a student at the Martial Arts Academy. I wanted to learn to do somersaults and walk across tightropes like the three boy acrobats. Would they teach me?

I was bursting with excitement when I rang Big Aunt's bell, dying to tell her about the performance I had just seen. But she was not alone.

"Where have you been? I was worried sick about you," she said, her gentle face looking strained.

4

"Sorry! I was watching an acrobatic show in the park—" I stopped when I saw there was a man in her sitting room. He was powerfully built and wore a black jacket with a mandarin collar.

"Let me introduce you," Big Aunt said in her polite voice. "This is my niece, Ye Xian. And this is Master CY Wu, who has just returned to Shanghai after visiting his family in Nan Tian. He and I are from the same island. We've been friends since kindergarten but he has been away in America. Master Wu tells me that my godmother, Grandma Liu, broke her leg last week and is asking for me. He and I are taking the train to Nan Tian first thing tomorrow morning."

I smiled feebly at the stranger sitting on the couch, and he nodded his head in acknowledgment. I was annoyed. Afternoons were supposed to be my time alone with Big Aunt. Every day after school, she and I would talk in English for half an hour. Then she'd show me different characters, which I had to translate into English. If I got them right, she would reward me with a sesame pancake or pork dumplings. Big Aunt was a fabulous cook, but obviously there wouldn't be any lessons or treats today. In addition to that, she was leaving for Nan Tian in the morning, and I knew I'd miss her terribly while she was away.

Master Wu looked like a professional athlete. The muscles of his upper arms bulged under his long-sleeved jacket. Every gesture he made suggested coordination, power and agility. He smiled at me.

Big Aunt could see that I was put out. "Master Wu is an

expert in *kung fu*. I said I'd give him painting lessons and he will teach me self-defense." A warm look passed between them. I got up and muttered that I ought to be going.

"Don't go yet!" Big Aunt said. "Master Wu's English is actually better than mine. He moved to California with his uncle when he was eight and lived there for a long time before he came back to China. How about the three of us having a conversation in English today? Will you begin, Master Wu?"

"Okay!" Master Wu agreed amiably. "Since we are speaking English, I think your niece should first be given an English name."

"What do you suggest?" Big Aunt asked Master Wu.

"Your aunt tells me that your mother died when you were five years old," Master Wu said to me. "Have you heard of the Cinderella story?"

"Of course!" I said.

"But do you know that the Cinderella story was printed in China during the Tang dynasty and first came out twelve hundred years ago?" Master Wu asked. "The little girl in the Chinese version has the same surname as you: Ye. Your given name is also the same: Xian. Amazing, isn't it?"

I was interested despite myself. "Did the Tang dynasty Chinese Cinderella also have a stepmother who was mean to her and a fairy godmother who looked out for her?" I asked.

"Instead of a fairy godmother, the Chinese Cinderella had a magic fish that protected her. But she did have a wicked stepmother who was very mean. Why do you ask?" Master Wu said.

"Do you have a stepmother?"

"Sort of." I looked at my aunt, wondering whether I should tell him more.

"Her father is Ye Jia-lin, my younger brother," Big Aunt explained. "Her mother was my best friend. So, besides being my niece, Ye Xian is also my goddaughter. We shared a room in my brother's house before his latest girlfriend moved in three years ago. She and I don't get along. I like reading, music and art, and she is only interested in jewelry, playing mah-jong and shopping. That's why I moved out last year."

"What do you call your father's girlfriend?" Master Wu asked me.

"Father told me to call her Niang—" I began.

"I've never liked you calling her Niang," Big Aunt interrupted heatedly. " 'Niang' is another term for 'mama.' If that woman is your mama, then what about your real mama? As far as I'm concerned, you have one mama and will always have only one real mama. Unfortunately, she died! That woman and your father aren't even married!"

"So what should I call her?"

"Call her 'Father's New Woman'!"

"How can I?" I said. "I can't say, 'Good morning, Father's New Woman. How are you today?' They'd kill me."

"It worries me that you'll be under the thumb of someone like her for the rest of your life." From outside came the sound of hammering as workers erected wooden arches for the parade to celebrate the Japanese takeover of Singapore. "History will repeat itself, just like the Cinderella story in the English version, Chinese version or any other version."

"Many of my friends tell me it's fashionable to have an English name as well as a Chinese name nowadays," I said, changing the subject. "I'd *love* to have an English name."

"I think Cinderella is perfect for you," Master Wu said. "It's the English equivalent of your Chinese name, Ye Xian!"

"Yes!" Big Aunt agreed. "*Chinese* Cinderella—but that's such a mouthful. Why don't we just use the initials and call you CC?"

And that is how I got my English name, CC.

CHAPTER 2

Chinese Zodiac

OW, LET'S BEGIN," said Big Aunt. I took my usual seat at the round dining table, which Big Aunt also used as her writing desk. Her sitting room was sparsely but elegantly furnished, with tatami mats on a wooden parquet floor, floor-to-ceiling bookshelves, large windows shaded by bamboo screens, a comfortable couch and two cozy armchairs. Pots of chrysanthemums dotted the room, and two large black-and-white ink paintings hung on the wall.

Big Aunt sat next to me and poured a little water on the ink stone, then made fresh ink by grinding a stick of charcoal against the stone's surface. She dipped a brush in the ink and quickly wrote a number of characters in our exercise book. They were so easy, I felt insulted.

"I know these words! I'm not three years old! I'm twelve!"

"*Xiao bao bei*, my precious little treasure!" Big Aunt said patiently. "*Yu su bu da!* More haste, less speed! Just read them aloud and translate them into English!"

I sighed and rolled my eyes to the ceiling. "They're all animals: the rat, ox, tiger, rabbit, dragon, snake, horse, goat, monkey, rooster, dog and pig." Suddenly I caught on. "But these are the signs of the zodiac. I know them! I'm a horse."

"Yes, *xiao bao bei*! But do you know that the Chinese zodiac has twelve-year cycles? It starts with the rat and ends with the pig. After that, the cycle starts again with the rat."

"Why is the rat always first?"

"Legend has it that Buddha wanted to start a calendar to keep track of time," Big Aunt explained. "He summoned all the animals and announced that the first twelve would be included in the Chinese zodiac. The rat came first, the pig last, and all the other animals came in between. Each animal was given a year of its own. For instance, people born in the year of the rat would adopt the personality traits of the rat."

"Who would want to be like a rat?"

"A person has no choice in that matter," Master Wu said. "Actually, I was born in the year of the rat and am now forty-two years old. Can you figure out when I was born, CC?"

I had to think. "Since it is 1942, you must have been born in 1900. Is that right, Master Wu?"

"One hundred percent correct!" Master Wu concurred. "Let me tell you something else. Your Big Aunt was also born in the year of the rat."

"Mama told me I was born in the year of the horse," I said.

"How old am I, Master Wu?"

Master Wu's eyes were bright. "The horse is the seventh animal on the zodiac, and 1906, 1918 and 1930 were all horse years. Since you don't look thirty-six or twenty-four years old, my logic tells me that you were born in 1930."

"What are horse people like?" I asked.

"Horse people are quick-witted and adventurous," Big Aunt said with a smile. "Most compatible with those born in the year of the tiger. Here is a chart for you to take home. Have fun with it at school. Your friends will be so impressed when you tell them what they are like and who they can be friends with. Now I have something else for you."

Quickly, Big Aunt wrote another two characters in the book.

"Easy again," I said. "These mean bear and cat."

"Yes," Big Aunt said. "But they also have another meaning. It's a riddle. . . . Master Wu, will you give CC a hint?"

Master Wu had moved to the window. He produced a faded photograph from his wallet. It was a picture of him standing next to a giant panda. The panda was pushing a basketball into a specially constructed hoop halfway up a tree.

"This is Mei Mei, Master Wu's pet," said Big Aunt.

I stared at the photo in disbelief as the truth slowly dawned. "The characters for bear and cat can also mean giant panda!" I exclaimed.

"Yes, *xiao bao bei*," Big Aunt said. "You've solved the riddle. Master Wu has a giant panda as a pet."

"Where is your panda, Master Wu?" I asked breathlessly. "May I see it?"

Master Wu shook his head. "Mei Mei hates the city. She lives in the mountain forests of Nan Tian Island, where there are plenty of bamboo leaves to eat."

I looked at the adorable panda's white face with dark circles around her eyes. "Will she know you when you see her again?"

"Of course! I've raised her since she was a pink baby, almost hairless, lying all soft and helpless in the palm of my hand."

I looked at his hand and tried to imagine the tiny baby panda. "How did you find her?"

Master Wu settled back on the couch, and I sat beside him. Big Aunt poured hot water from a thermos into three blue-and-white china teacups, added a pinch of tea leaves to each and covered the cups with matching lids for the tea to brew.

"Four years ago," Master Wu began, "I was visiting my uncle in Sichuan Province in the southwest. His house was high in the mountains, near a misty, cloud-covered bamboo forest. One morning while I was out walking, I heard a shot and some hunters crashing through the trees. Then I came upon a terrible sight—a giant panda, mortally wounded. I hid and watched the hunters tie up the body and carry it away."

I felt sick. The thought of such a beautiful animal being slaughtered revolted me. "Why did they do it?" I asked.

Big Aunt looked sad. "Panda skin and meat fetch a high price. The paws especially have medicinal value. Many people think they're a great delicacy."

"After the hunters had gone," Master Wu continued, "I searched for the dead panda's den and found it in the hollow stump of a fir tree, lined with twigs, wood chips, leaves and stalks of bamboo. Then I heard the sound of an animal squealing and saw the baby panda. It was still pink, with just the slightest covering of white fur. . . ."

"Was it inside the den?" I could hardly bear to think of the baby panda losing its mother in such a brutal way.

"No, it was lying on a pile of dead leaves a little distance away. Pandas often carry their cubs in their mouths when they search for food. The cub probably dropped out of its mother's mouth when she was shot."

Master Wu took a sip of tea. I was sitting on the edge of the couch, hanging on to every word.

"I carried the baby panda back in my coat to our home in Nan Tian. My mother's neighbor is Liu Nai Nai, Grandma Liu. She often rescues animals, and I knew she would give the panda the best chance of survival. We called the panda Mei Mei, which means 'beautiful sister.' Grandma Liu and I fed her powdered milk with a baby's bottle until she was old enough to eat bamboo leaves on her own. I taught her to turn somersaults, climb trees and play basketball. She's very smart. Eventually, when she was big enough, we released her into the forest. But, even now, she often visits the house and comes to me when I call her name."

Big Aunt placed a pot of water over the stove. I saw that she had prepared sweet sesame balls as well as anise-flavored tea eggs. The three of us sat around her kitchen table drinking jasmine tea and eating her delicious snacks. I wanted to stay there forever.

"Please let me stay here tonight," I begged. "I don't want to go to Father's house and face Niang. I'm going to miss you so much."

"Has it been bad?" Big Aunt asked. She reached for my hand.

I realized my fingers were clenched.

"Niang hates me!" I said. "Everything I do is wrong. She doesn't even call me by my name anymore! It's always 'you loathsome creature' or 'you disgusting troublemaker.' I just want to be with you."

Big Aunt looked at Master Wu before turning back to me. "Tonight is my last night in Shanghai. I want to be with you too. Why don't you phone your father and ask to stay with me?"

When I called, Father sounded preoccupied but agreed that I could stay. I didn't want the night to end.

CHAPTER 3

Abandoned and Homeless

KNEW IT WAS GOING to be bad as soon as I came home from school. Ah Sun, one of our maids, said, "Your niang wishes to see you. She is waiting in the living room."

I had dreaded this moment all day, and now it was upon me. I gritted my teeth and tried to remember what Big Aunt had said that morning: "You can be anybody you wish to be as long as you study hard. Knowledge is power. Don't let anyone drag you down. *Zi qiang bu xi*—motivate yourself to work hard and be strong always! Have faith in yourself, because I'll always believe in you."

"Where is Father?" I asked Ah Sun.

"He's taking a nap in his bedroom."

I took a deep breath, straightened my shoulders and went into the living room.

"Good afternoon, Niang."

Niang sat on the couch filing her bright red, perfectly manicured nails. She gave me a quick glance. Her back was stiff and her eyes hard. She reminded me of a beast of prey readying for the kill. A voice in my head kept saying, *Be careful!*

"Where were you last night?" she said sharply.

"At my aunt's apartment."

"Who gave you permission?"

"Father did. I telephoned him."

"Come here!" she commanded.

I approached her gingerly, trembling with fear. Without getting up, she extended her arm and slapped my cheek. It was so hard, I almost fell.

"Why did you slap me? What did I do wrong?"

"Shut up!" she shrieked, slapping me again. "This is for staying out all night without permission!"

"That's not true!" I cried. "I did get permission! From my father!"

"What about me?" she screamed. "Did you get permission from me? Of course not! You think I'm nobody, don't you? You and that slut of an aunt of yours!"

"Don't call my aunt a slut!"

"Who are you to tell me what to call your aunt? You miserable nuisance! I'll call her whatever I want!"

"If anyone is a slut," I said recklessly, "it's you!"

This time Niang did not slap me but placed her cold hands around my throat. I felt her long, sharp nails digging into my neck as she squeezed with all her might. Desperate for air, I wriggled and kicked in a furious attempt to get away. I was certain that she was going to kill me.

I had a crazy vision of my limp and lifeless body lying in a child's coffin, and of Big Aunt's tear-stained face. My legs began to quiver, and the floor felt soft under my feet. My nostrils were filled with the terrifying fragrance of her perfume.

With one desperate effort, I opened my mouth wide, pulled wildly at her hair and sank my teeth into her bare arm.

She released her choke hold with a yelp of pain and stared at her arm. I felt something warm and wet trickling down my chin. Gasping for air, I wiped my streaming nose with the back of my hand. Bright red blood smeared across my wrist. Her slaps had caused my nose to bleed.

My legs were shaking so violently, I could hardly stand. I could not believe what I had done. In a trembling voice, I stammered, "I'm sorry I bit you. Please forgive me! I didn't mean to hurt you. It's just that I couldn't breathe."

She did not look at me as she pronounced the dreadful words. "Since you are not happy here, get out! I'm going to tell your father that you behaved like a wild dog! You don't belong in this house!"

She went upstairs. The silence was ominous. Then my father rushed downstairs in a cold fury.

"How dare you bite your mother!" he demanded.

When I tried to explain that I was defending myself, he refused to listen. "Obviously you're not happy living here," he said coldly.

"She called Big Aunt a slut!"

"Did you or did you not bite her?"

"She was choking me to death!"

"You are the child, and she is your niang! She has every right to punish you in whatever way she wishes."

"Even if she kills me?"

"Don't be ridiculous! Of course she's not going to kill you! She has your welfare at heart at all times. After all, she's your niang."

Then I said something awful. I was so tired of her malice and his hypocrisy. Even as the words came bursting out of my mouth, I knew that my life was doomed. "You and I both know she is not my niang. She hates me! No, Father! She is not my niang and has never been my niang! She is just your New Woman!"

"How dare you! Get out of my house this minute! Get out and never come back!" He was in such a rage that he grabbed the back of my school uniform and lifted me off the floor as if I were a kitten. Then he marched to the back door, dumped me outside and slammed the door behind me.

On the streets of Shanghai, Japanese soldiers were everywhere, in their belted uniforms and peaked caps, their bayonets flashing. I saw a headline on a newsstand as I walked by: USA AND BRITAIN COWERING UNDER THE MIGHT OF JAPAN AND GERMANY. The war hit me in a way I'd not experienced before. Now I was on the streets too, unprotected and on my own like thousands of homeless refugees. What would become of me?

I shivered. My school uniform was made of thick navy blue wool, but I had neither a coat nor a sweater. Everyone had somewhere to go. I was starting to panic.

Suddenly there was a commotion. Two Japanese soldiers were attacking a paperboy, kicking, slapping and abusing him verbally for not bowing as they walked by. The terrified boy begged for mercy, and the soldiers eventually swaggered off after kicking down his stand and scattering what was left to the wind. Like the other bystanders, I could only watch in fear and silence, keeping my eyes down. The front page of a copy of *China Daily* landed at my feet. Its headline proclaimed: A SECOND PEARL HARBOR? BRITISH FORCES COLLAPSE IN SINGAPORE AFTER ONLY ONE DAY OF FIGHTING.

Motorcars, trams, pedicabs, rickshaws and bicycles whizzed by. I was caught up in the life of the street, but belonged nowhere. A father and daughter dressed in rags crouched on the pavement. Around the child's neck was a sign: FOR SALE! MY NAME IS LUO YING. I AM EIGHT YEARS OLD. For a second our eyes met, and the girl thrust her thin dirty hand into my face. I pulled away and ran down an alley, the blood pounding in my ears. Had the world gone mad?

Without thinking about where I was going, I ended up outside Big Aunt's apartment. How could Father have done this to me, his daughter? And Mama, why did she have to die? I couldn't see through my tears. How fast fortune changes! Yesterday I was still the lucky child enjoying an acrobatic show in the park. . . .

Acrobatic show! I remembered the card given to me by the boy acrobat. I plunged my hand into my pocket, dizzy with relief.

LONG XIA HUI　龍俠會

DRAGON SOCIETY OF WANDERING KNIGHTS
Martial Arts Academy
Plaza in Du Mei Gardens &
2200 Avenue Pétain, Shanghai

We help the oppressed and downtrodden.
We show the *tao*—way—to those who are lost.
Martial Arts. Judo. Karate. Boxing. Kickboxing. Acrobatics.
Chinese Classics. Poetry. Calligraphy. Brush Painting. Music.

With a rush of hope, I sprinted into the park.

It was completely deserted. Yesterday's stage had been removed, and the acrobats had vanished. I felt limp. This was bad. Very bad. Big Aunt was gone. The acrobats were gone. For a fleeting moment, I considered creeping back to Father's house and begging him for forgiveness, but the thought of Niang overwhelmed me with dread. Perhaps it would be better to end the misery and die.

I looked at the sycamore tree next to me, searching for a foothold to climb to the top and jump to my death. There, near a clump of leaves, I saw a row of ants struggling up a slippery rock face. The ants' determination gave me courage. If the ants could survive, so could I.

For a long time, I sat by the tree in silence, trying to picture Big Aunt's expression when she first taught me the proverb *Bai zhe bu nao!* Stick to your goal despite a hundred setbacks! I was far away in my thoughts when I heard a gardener clipping the lilac bushes nearby.

"Where's your mother?" he said. "It's really not safe for a little girl your age to be hanging around a park all by herself like this. Don't you know there's a war going on?"

"Actually, I was looking for the acrobats who performed here yesterday. Are they coming back today?"

"Their permit only allows them to perform in the Plaza three times a year. Their next appearance will be during the Dragon Boat Festival in a few months' time."

"Where can I find them?" I couldn't conceal my disappointment.

He shrugged. "How would I know? Shanghai is a big place. . . ." Then he saw my tears. "Now, now! Don't cry. Tell you what. Occasionally, I've seen those boys working at a bookstall in the bazaar behind that row of tall trees. Why don't you see if they're there today?"

In the bazaar, hawkers were selling toys, delicate paper cutouts, crickets, birds in cages, fans, fireworks, stick incense, fruits, ice cream, preserved plums, dates, even dried squid and herbal medicines from makeshift stands. I was overwhelmed by the smells and colors, the hustle and bustle of buying and selling and bargaining. Finally, I spotted the bookstall. A white-haired woman was arranging hundreds of new and used *kung fu* novels on racks that resembled window shutters. A sign said: MARTIAL ARTS ACADEMY AND BOOKSTALL. BOOKS FOR SALE OR LOAN.

I chose a book, *Warriors from the Marsh of Mount Liang*, sat down and flipped open the pages. Printed in black and white on cheap rice paper, it told the story of a group of idealistic men in the twelfth century who formed a secret brotherhood to right the wrongs of those who were unjustly accused.

The woman came and sat next to me. "This book is based on a famous novel written by Shi Nan-an six hundred years ago during the Ming dynasty. It has been adapted for children and has lots of drawings. We have many young customers your age." She smiled at me so kindly that I felt brave enough to speak.

"I know you!" I burst forth. "Are you the leader of the acrobats who performed at Du Mei Gardens yesterday?"

"You're right!" she smiled warmly. "Here comes one of my boys now!"

There were the lilting tones of a bamboo flute, and the boy who had given me his card pushed through the crowd. I hardly recognized him without his satin costume, but I remembered his face. His eyes were laughing, and I saw that they were different colors: one dark brown and the other blue.

CHAPTER 4

New Friends

HE BOY HELD OUT his hand. "*Ni hau*—how are you? You're the girl who keeps coins in her ears! I was hoping to see you again. I'm David Black, and this is my teacher, Wu Nai Nai, Grandma Wu."

My heart pounded, but I managed to get up from the bench. First I bowed to Grandma Wu, then I shook David's hand.

"I'm Ye Xian, but my English name is CC." I tried to keep my voice steady. "Your show was marvelous."

"It wasn't too bad, was it?" David replied with a big grin. "I see you're reading one of my favorite books, *Warriors from the Marsh of Mount Liang*."

"It's my favorite too!" I said.

"I like it because the Mount Liang warriors dared to stand up for their beliefs," David said. "If you read just one book in your life, it should be this one!"

23

"I wish I could be a Mount Liang warrior," I said.

"You can be! Grandma Wu, do you think members of our society are as brave as the warriors of Mount Liang?"

"We try to be," Grandma Wu said. "Many of the fighting techniques I've taught you are named after characters in this novel. Why don't you show CC some of your *kung fu* moves?"

"I have a better idea!" David said. "May I invite CC to the academy this Sunday? That's the day of my match."

"I don't see why not." Grandma Wu turned to me. "David's going to fight the junior boxing champion of Shanghai in an exhibition match at noon this Sunday. He'll be using classic *kung fu* moves such as Wu Song's 'Step Back and Ride the Tiger' and Li Kui's 'Two-handed Axe.'"

"I've always wanted to learn *kung fu*," I said wistfully. Everything was happening so fast that I felt confused. Just an hour ago, I was at the bottom of an abyss. My life seemed full of darkness, and my heart was aching so much that I yearned to die. But hope must have been lurking somewhere all along. I had a sudden longing for the place I used to call home when my mother was still alive. Were my worries truly over, or would Grandma Wu turn me away too, just as Father had done when he slammed the door behind me?

Some of my pain must have shown on my face. "What is it, CC? Is something troubling you?" Grandma Wu looked at me with concern.

Her tone was so sympathetic that tears came to my eyes. "My aunt left for Nan Tian Island early this morning. I had a quarrel with my stepmother this afternoon, and my father threw me out of their house. I don't know where to go tonight. . . ." My voice broke, and to my embarrassment, I started to weep again.

Grandma Wu put her arm around my shoulders. "Don't cry! You're among friends. Let me get something straight, though. Did you say that your aunt left for Nan Tian early this morning? It so happens that I was born on that island and grew up there. What's your aunt's name?"

When I told her it was Ye Jia-ming, her eyes opened wide. "What a small world! I do believe that you and I have *yuan fen* together. Just like the poem says:

> *People with* yuan fen *are destined to like one another;*
> *Friendship develops even if a thousand miles apart.*
> *But should* yuan fen *be absent between two individuals,*
> *They will remain strangers despite sitting face-to-face.*

"Here! Dry your tears. Take a deep breath and tell us your story."

So I told Grandma Wu and David about the quarrel with my stepmother and my father's anger when I called her his "New Woman." I had never revealed my painful family situation to anyone at school before and felt uneasy discussing it with these two strangers I had just met. "Now I have nowhere to go," I said, hanging my head.

Grandma Wu and David were silent at first. Then Grandma Wu gently lifted my face and said, "Your aunt's godmother, Liu

Nai Nai, Grandma Liu, and I lived across the street from each other in Nan Tian when we were children! My son and I still own that house. We've been friends for more than fifty years. She taught everyone on the island how to swim, including my son and your aunt. I remember little Ye Jia-ming well. She and my son used to build sand castles on the beach hour after hour. In those days, she wore pigtails and liked to draw pictures on the sand with a stick!"

As she spoke, a thought struck me. "My aunt went to Nan Tian with a friend whom I met yesterday. His name is CY Wu. Is he your son?"

"Yes! My son has wanted to marry your aunt Ye Jia-ming all his life. Unfortunately, your grandfather had promised her to someone else when she was still a baby. Your aunt had no say in the matter. As you know, her arranged marriage was a disaster and she's now divorced—"

A jangle of sounds interrupted our conversation, as a band of roving musicians pushed through the crowd: six elderly men playing drum, cymbal, *erhu* (violin), gong, flute and castanets. Their music was so loud and distracting that we couldn't talk. I pressed my fingers against my ears and looked around. Wafting through the air was a delicious aroma. Hunger pangs gripped me, and I remembered that I had eaten nothing since noon. A food seller opposite us was sautéing pork and noodles in a giant wok perched above a portable charcoal stove. To his right was a fruit vendor with piles of persimmons, mandarin oranges, jujubes, dates, apples and pears. To his left squatted a shoemaker

totally absorbed in sewing on the sole of a shoe made of cloth.
Right next to our stall was a sign that said:

YI JING IS A BOOK OF MAGIC
I USE IT TO TELL YOUR FORTUNE

Under it, a fortune-teller was speaking intently to a female customer. They were so close, I could hear part of their conversation. In his hands, he held a bundle of sticks and a book with a
black cover.

The sight of the fortune-teller reminded me of my own mis-
fortune and desperate future. Terrified of spending the night
alone on the streets of Shanghai, I dropped to my knees in front
of Grandma Wu. "Please don't send me back to my stepmother,"
I pleaded. "Take me home with you and let me join your society. I've nowhere to go and don't know what to do."

Grandma Wu pulled me to my feet and held me again.
"Stop worrying, CC! I wouldn't *dream* of abandoning you.
Grandma Liu and I promised each other years ago that we
would always *tong gun gong ku* —share bitter and sweet—and
tong zhou gong ji— stick together through thick and thin. That's
the sort of friendship we share. You are the niece of my best
friend's goddaughter. You are also homeless, beset with perils
and in desperate need of help. Besides, I do believe that you and
I have *yuan fen* between us. Lots and lots of *yuan fen*. No question about it. You are definitely coming back with us to the
academy!"

CHAPTER 5

Wu Shu Xue Shiao—
Martial Arts Academy

HE ACADEMY was a converted warehouse on Avenue Pétain in the French Concession. It was divided into two wings with a courtyard in between. The rooms were enormous, and Grandma Wu had partitioned them into smaller areas with bamboo paneling. The left wing consisted of classrooms, study areas and a gymnasium. Dormitories and living quarters were in the right wing. There was hardly any furniture, and the windows were covered with rattan screens. The quiet, immaculate interior was in striking contrast to the noise and activity of Avenue Pétain. I discovered later that Grandma Wu, Master Wu and the three boy acrobats were the only ones living there. The rest of the students and staff of the academy had been evacuated to Chungking* two months ago when the Japanese took control of Shanghai.

*See Historical Note, page 225.

David stayed close to my side, but still I felt nervous and shy. Two other acrobat boys were in the kitchen wrapping dumplings. One was tall, muscular and gangly. The other was short and skinny and wore glasses. When we entered, they both sprang to their feet.

"Marat and Sam," Grandma Wu began, "come here and meet CC."

"You don't know me, but I know you," I said shyly. "Yesterday I watched you cycling and juggling balls on the tightrope. You were wonderful!"

"Marat Yoshida, the tightrope walker, that's me!" The taller boy smiled.

"I'd rather be known as Top-of-the-Line Performer Sam Eisner," the shorter boy quipped, laughing at his own joke. "But aren't you the girl who keeps coins in her ears?"

"I think she'd rather be known as the niece of Grandma Liu's goddaughter," said David.

"You don't mean Grandma Fish!" Marat said.

"Grandma Liu is my aunt's godmother. She has broken her leg, and my aunt has gone with Master Wu to Nan Tian to look after her," I said, pleased at the connections between us.

"What? Is she all right? How did she break her leg?" David asked anxiously.

"You know what a great swimmer Grandma Liu is and how she loves those dolphins of hers!" Grandma Wu took over. "Apparently, while she was playing with one of the dolphins, she lost her footing and fell from the boat. Don't forget that she's seventy-one now, and her bones are not as strong as they used to be—her leg simply snapped in two. I don't know the whole story, but I do know that the dolphin saved her life. Somehow it managed to push her all the way ashore."

"That's amazing!" I exclaimed. "Are dolphins really that smart?"

"Sure they are!" said David. "I once played football with a dolphin by tossing a bunch of seaweed back and forth! And last summer Grandma Liu taught one to walk on his tail. Dolphins love to play, and you can always tell when they are happy—they leap up and splash back into the water over and over again. Just like me when I throw my cap repeatedly in the air because things are going well." He grinned at me.

"So you've actually played with real dolphins!" I said enviously. "I've only seen pictures of them."

"When Marat and I went to Nan Tian with Grandma Wu, we spent so much time with Grandma Liu and her dolphins in the water that we started calling her Grandma Fish," David explained.

"I had measles," Sam said, wanting to join in. "So I stayed in Shanghai with Master Wu. Are you coming to live here?" He looked curiously at my school uniform.

"CC will be staying with us tonight and probably longer," said Grandma Wu. "She's here to learn *kung fu*. David, please take CC to Miss Cheng's old bedroom upstairs and show her around while I help Marat and Sam with dinner."

"Thank you, Grandma Wu," I said. So much had happened

since I left Big Aunt's apartment that morning. I could hardly think clearly, let alone plan for my future. How long would I be allowed to stay here? How would I earn my keep? I decided to simply do what I was told for the time being.

"Isn't David an English name?" I asked as we climbed the stairs to the spare bedroom. "Do you have a Chinese name too?"

David laughed. "Of course I have a Chinese name. It's Da-wei, which means 'big comfort.' My father was American and gave me the name David when I was born. My Chinese mother translated it to Da-wei. The two names sound almost the same in the Shanghai dialect. When people ask me my name, I say Da-wei unless I want to know that person better. Then I say David."

"What's your nickname?"

"What makes you think I have a nickname?" he said, smiling. "Do you have a nickname? Tell me yours first!"

"My best friend at school calls me Scholar Ye. She says my nose is always buried in a book. Yesterday, Master Wu gave me CC as my English name. It's really another nickname because the initials stand for Chinese Cinderella."

"I like it. My nickname is Black Whirlwind."

"Black Whirlwind! That's the nickname of Liu Kui, the character from *Warriors from the Marsh of Mount Liang*, isn't it? Wasn't he the fastest *kung fu* warrior of his generation? Who called you that?"

"Master Wu! It's appropriate because my English surname is Black!"

"You must be great at *kung fu* to be called Black Whirlwind."

I was full of questions about the academy and Master Wu as we stepped onto the landing. David first showed me the enormous dorm room he shared with Marat and Sam. There were at least twenty beds, but only three were in use. Beside each bed was a nightstand and a bamboo screen for privacy. David walked past the door of a similar room and said, "This used to be the girls' dorm, but they've all gone to Chungking. The spare bedroom you've been given used to belong to Miss Cheng, the calligraphy teacher. But she went west too, and it's been empty since."

When we finished putting sheets and pillowcases on my bed, I had a good look around. There was a small bookcase above the bed, as well as a skylight, a writing desk and two small chairs. The large glass windows were covered with rattan screens.

"How long have you lived with Grandma Wu? Where are your parents?"

"My father and my mother are dead." David's voice became quiet and strained. "My mother was arrested by the Japanese secret police on the same day they killed my father. She died in jail a few days later. I've lived with Grandma Wu and Master Wu for two months. Ever since Pearl Harbor Day, December seventh of last year."

I was shocked. "I'm so sorry. . . ." My words seemed inadequate.

David shrugged. "Don't be. Your story is just as sad. Everyone ends up here for a reason. Grandma Wu and Master Wu move around the country and the *jiang hu*—rivers and lakes—helping unwanted children like us. They teach us the *tao*, true way to live. They give us hope."

I started to feel excited. My old life was fading away, my new life full of possibility. "What's it like living here? What do you do all day?"

"Grandma Wu makes us practice martial arts two hours a day, and we still have to go to school full-time, study the classics and learn thirty new Chinese characters a week. I wish I had more time to play my flute, but I love it here. Master Wu says that if you like what you do, there isn't any difference between work and play."

"Is Master Wu an athlete? He looks like a professional boxer or weight lifter."

"He's amazingly talented. He can run a mile in less than four and a half minutes, lift weights that are more than two hundred fifty pounds, swim sixty meters underwater in less than two minutes and jump over hurdles five feet high. But his *kung fu* moves are the best of all. When he lived in Los Angeles, he even defeated the flyweight boxing champion of California!"

We had dinner in the kitchen, the five of us sitting around the same round table where Marat and Sam had been wrapping dumplings earlier. I thought how wonderful it was to be eating the food that the two boys had prepared with their own hands:

so different from my father's house, where every meal was cooked and served by the maids. Besides dumplings, there was a plate of fried noodles and a large bowl of vegetable soup. Grandma Wu placed the different dishes on a small turntable set in the middle and told us to help ourselves. We used chopsticks and plates for the food but drank the soup out of small bowls.

The boys laughed and joked throughout the meal. I wanted so much to join in.

When we were clearing the table, David whispered, "Don't worry! Grandma Wu likes you! Everything will be all right!"

Grandma Wu smiled gently. "Even though you have suffered much, CC, there's always someone who has suffered more. It's certainly not fair that your own father should kick you out of your house, but there are people who have not only lost their parents but were kicked out of their country as well!"

I was shocked. "Who's that?"

"You'll find out!"

"I'm so grateful to you for taking me in," I said. "It also means a lot to me to eat Marat and Sam's dumplings."

"Nothing cements friendship like something cooked by a friend," Grandma Wu replied. And I vowed to myself then and there that I would learn to cook so I could return the favor.

After dinner, Grandma Wu led us to an alcove that was separated from the rest of the living room by special folding screens. Hanging on the wall was a scroll with two large Chinese characters: *Fu Dao*, the Way of Buddha. Below the scroll was an exquisite bonsai tree resting on an antique altar table. Two elaborately carved sandalwood boxes were on either side of the bonsai tree. On the front of each were three Chinese characters: *Gu Yi He*, Memory Vision Box, on the left; and *Wei Lei He*, Future Vision Box, on the right. Otherwise the alcove was bare apart from a small stool.

Grandma Wu gave each of us a red candle in a bamboo basket and told us to remain silent and to speak only after lighting our candles. She turned off the lights, lit a candle for herself and placed it on the floor in front of her. Then she sat on the stool with the three boys and me in a semicircle around her. It was strange to see the boys quiet after all the talking and joking at dinner.

I could see Grandma Wu's white hair and refined features dimly outlined in the quivering candlelight. Her expression was serene and thoughtful. I half closed my eyes to concentrate. Within a few minutes, a sense of calm flowed through me. I knew I was entering an extraordinary world: a unique spiritual shelter.

Grandma Wu began to speak, her voice clear and calm. "We are gathered here this evening to welcome CC Ye, the niece of Grandma Liu's goddaughter, Ye Jia-ming. The Dragon Society is a branch of the Shaolin Association of Wandering Knights that has existed in China for more than fourteen hundred years. Our members have a tradition of helping those who have suffered unjustly and have nobody to turn to. During times of war, ma children must fend for themselves. We are here for them.

"A large part of China, including our great city of Shanghai, is occupied by Japanese invaders. Times are difficult. No one knows how long this will last.

"I want you to understand that both happiness and unhappiness arise from within. A person's strength lies in her desire to do the right thing by her conscience. I know that we all have different religious backgrounds. David is Christian, Sam is Jewish, Marat is Muslim and I am Buddhist. As a Buddhist, I consider God to be the same as Heaven, and life as a *tao*, a journey that takes us step by step toward the goal of Heaven. To reach Heaven is beyond our power. Our goal is to try to get there.

"You, CC, have expressed a wish to join the Dragon Society. We are willing to consider this, but membership depends on merit. If you are found worthy, you will be invited to join. When you join, you will have to swear allegiance to our society for the rest of your life. Are you prepared to do this?"

Mindful that I was not to speak without lighting my candle, I nodded my head solemnly. Inside I was feeling a little uneasy. *The rest of my life* is a long commitment, I told myself. Besides, ¦on't really know anything about the Dragon Society as yet.

¦You are forbidden to reveal anything that happens in the ¦Candlelight meetings such as this must be kept secret at ¦Grandma Wu said. "We are living in dangerous times, ¦room for error. The enemy is all around us."

¦turned to face me.

¦ust reveal yourself to us, CC. Tell us the

story of your life so that we will get to know you from the heart. See these two boxes next to the bonsai tree? The one on the left is a door to your past. The one on the right is a window to your future. Here is a match. Light your candle. Now that your candle is lit, you may speak."

I moved to the center of the circle, where Grandma Wu handed me the box marked *Gu Yi He* and indicated that I should look into the two holes cut out at eye level. All I saw at first was a jumble of black dots against a white, brightly lit background.

"You are looking into a Memory Vision Box, CC," Grandma Wu said quietly. "Our academy places as much emphasis on *dyana*, meditation, as physical training. We aim to match the expansion of your mind with the development of your body. We need to understand your past so that we can blend the external with the internal parts of your nature.

"Look deeply into the box! The dots you see will rearrange themselves every time you press the button on the left. Take your time! Tell us what you see."

Even before Grandma Wu finished speaking, I had already pressed the button on the left side of the box. The dots organized themselves into a picture, like an old family photo in black and white. There was a large bed on which sat a family of three dressed in silk pajamas: a father, mother and a young child. The mother had the child in her arms, and I could see the father holding up a picture of a horse. I suppressed a gasp when I saw their faces.

"I see my father and mother!" I said, overcome with emotion. "And me! It was a long time ago, when Mama was still alive. She used to read to me before putting me to bed. Sometimes Papa would sit with us. I remember that evening: Mama told me I was born in the year of the horse, and Papa showed me what a horse looked like. He tried to write the word 'horse' with a brush, but ink dripped onto the sheet and Mama scolded him.

"Mama!" I whispered as I stared hungrily into the box. "Papa!"

Neither of my parents looked at me. I pressed my face against the box and felt a terrible ache inside, half pain and half nostalgia. For the first time since Mama's death, I spoke openly of her. I told Grandma Wu and the boys of my mother's last illness and the nightmare of her death; the anguish of meeting Papa's girlfriend and being forced to call her Niang; the increasing coldness of my father and the knowledge that I had become a thorn in his side; the daily humiliation and incessant criticism at home. As the words tumbled out of my mouth, I felt a heavy weight gradually lift from my shoulders. I ended by telling them about the quarrel with Niang that had resulted in my being kicked out of my father's house. Tears flowed down my cheeks.

Suddenly the room was lit up with the light of three more candles, and the boys were kneeling in front of me. They held their candles aloft in their raised fists as they chanted in unison:

"We are members of the Dragon Society
We are the reincarnated Wandering Knights of Mount Liang

We help people seeking for truth to find the tao
We fight on behalf of those unjustly accused

"The yielding conquers the resistant
The soft vanquishes the hard
Overcome the opponent by stillness
Subdue the enemy at the instant of attack
The one standing on tiptoe does not stand firm
The one taking the longest strides may not be the fastest

"United we stand till the end of our lives
In Unity there is Power"

An enormous sense of relief swept over me. For the first time since Niang came into my life, I was surrounded by people who were on my side. I was no longer alone! We bowed three times, first to the characters *Fu Dao*, then to Grandma Wu and finally to one another.

Grandma Wu's expression was fierce and compassionate at the same time. She looked ageless, like a female warrior, her eyes holding the suffering and wisdom of her years.

"Oh, CC!" she said tenderly. "Thank you for your moving words and for sharing your past with us. Tonight's ceremony marks a new beginning. Tomorrow you will start your apprenticeship and your life with us at our academy. If you do well, you will be asked to become a member. Meanwhile, we as a family welcome you. Besides your Big Aunt, you now have me as your grandmother, Master Wu as your second father and David, Sam and Marat as your brothers. Members of our society are linked to other like-minded people throughout the world. All of us believe in equality, democracy, morality, independence, justice and fair play. That is what we are fighting for.

"Chinese people now have the choice of resistance or submission to the Japanese occupation of our country. Our society has chosen to resist, so China can become free and independent one day. This is our sacred mission."

Grandma Wu handed me the second box, marked *Wei Lei He*, Future Vision Box. This time there were no eyeholes, but a decorative lid, which I opened. The box was divided into two chambers. The larger contained a red robe, a hat and a pair of sandals. Inside the smaller compartment was a tattered book bound in red cloth. A bundle of sticks, neatly tied with a cord, was attached to the book's spine.

"It looks very old," I said.

"This book was written more than three thousand years ago," she said. "It is called the Yi Jing, or Book of Changes. We Chinese believe that everything in the world changes with time. The only thing that does not change is that everything changes."

"I know about the Yi Jing!" I exclaimed. "At the bazaar this afternoon, the fortune-teller in the stall next to yours was fiddling with a bunch of sticks. I heard him tell a customer that the Yi Jing is a book of magic that can foretell everyone's future!"

"The Yi Jing is actually a book of wisdom," Grandma Wu said. "If I were to tell you that a mysterious stranger might visit

40

you tonight, there is nothing you can do about his visit but wait. The stranger may or may not arrive. This is called fate. Consulting the Yi Jing will not help in such an instance."

"But is it a book of magic?" I asked.

"Yes and no! There are times when we're uncertain as to what we should do, knowing that our fate hangs in the balance. But how do we know which is the right road to take and which the wrong? How do we make the correct choice? On those occasions, when we wish to decide our own future but are confused as to what to do, the Yi Jing can definitely be of help."

"Please, may I read it now?" I asked eagerly.

Grandma Wu smiled gently at the hunger in my eyes, but her voice was firm. "It is not the right time yet, CC," she said. "When that time comes, I will tell you."

I was desperate to open the book but knew I had to be patient. I kept silent but couldn't help wondering whether the boys had also looked into the two vision boxes at some point. If so, what had they seen? Had they been allowed to read the Yi Jing yet? What did it tell them about *their* future?

Waves of weariness suddenly swept over me, and I started to yawn. Soon everyone was yawning.

"Catching, isn't it?" Grandma Wu said with a smile. "It's been a long day! Especially for you, CC! This meeting is now over and you can all go to bed. Please blow out your candles. Even though there's no school tomorrow because it's Saturday, I expect to see the four of you downstairs in the kitchen at seven o'clock sharp."

CHAPTER 6

Kung Fu

 WOKE TO FIND A RAY of light from a skylight on my face and David standing over my bed. "Wake up, CC!" His hair was tousled as usual, his eyes eager. "It's seven o'clock and everyone's waiting for you."

For a moment, I couldn't work out where I was. With a dull thud, I remembered the events of the previous day. Had all of that happened in just one day? What did Father think when I didn't come home all night? I hadn't told him about Big Aunt leaving for Nan Tian Island. Would he assume I was staying with her? But as I relived how he had thrown me out of the house, my fear was replaced by anger. David must have sensed my somber mood, but he said nothing about it. "Hurry up! Grandma Wu wants you to get dressed and come downstairs as soon as possible," he urged as he left my room.

I knew I had overslept and jumped out of bed in a hurry. I had nothing else to wear so I put on my school uniform again.

Sam, Marat and David were already eating breakfast when I came to the table. The boys were dressed in identical dark blue cotton pants and black T-shirts. I apologized for being late and sat down at the place they had set for me between David and Sam. I was starving, and the simple breakfast of rice porridge, boiled peanuts and salted duck egg tasted wonderful.

"Where's Grandma Wu?" I asked between mouthfuls.

"She's watering her plants and feeding her pigeons," Marat said, scrutinizing a sheet of paper in front of him. "She's given us our chores for the week. David and CC are to plan next week's daily dinner menu, cook the meals and do the washing up. Sam and I have to do the laundry, water the plants, clean the toilets and sweep the rooms. Everybody helps to make lunch today."

"Oh, no!" Sam groaned. "I'd much rather cook than clean toilets!"

"I'll help clean the toilets if you teach me how to cook!" I suggested shyly. "Those dumplings last night were wonderful! What did you and Marat put in them?"

"Minced pork, ginger, scallions, water chestnuts and soya sauce," Sam listed. "Nothing to it. Cooking's easy!"

"Never trust a skinny cook!" said David, eyeing Sam's slender frame and laughing. "Let's stick to Grandma Wu's schedule. I can show you how to cook, CC."

"Does that mean you won't be helping me with the toilets?" Sam asked me.

"The truth is I don't know how to clean toilets either," I

said, feeling useless and dejected. "There were always servants in our house who did stuff like that. But I need to learn to clean toilets too. If you'll show me how, I'll do it for you."

"Okay! That's a deal!"

After we finished washing the dishes, Grandma Wu called us into the courtyard. She lined us up according to our height: David, Marat, Sam and me. Then she handed me a piece of paper. On it was the same poem that had been recited the night before.

"The boys already know this poem by heart," she said. "You need to learn it too, CC."

The four of us chanted in unison, "We are members of the Dragon Society . . ." until the end.

"Now let's show CC what you can do," Grandma Wu said to the boys.

They moved into position and started to stretch their limbs, turn somersaults, leapfrog over one another and dance on their toes while shadowboxing in the air.

While they were warming up, Grandma Wu told me, "My purpose in teaching you *kung fu* is to give you inner courage and self-confidence. You will learn to climb walls like a lizard, swim like a dolphin and run through fire without getting burned. Most important, you will learn about focusing the direction of your *Qi**, the powerful life force that exists within all living

*pronounced *chee*

things. Skill and power in *kung fu* come from channeling your *Qi* and transforming it into movement and fluidity. *Qi* is the foundation of a person's courage, will and perseverance."

As I was pondering Grandma Wu's words, she blew a whistle hanging around her neck. The boys stopped their exercises and raced to a bamboo pole that was leaning against a wall. Taking turns to hold the pole steady, they climbed to the top of the wall before jumping down and doing it all over again. Grandma Wu gradually decreased the angle between the pole and the wall. Finally, she removed the pole altogether. To my amazement, I saw them scaling the wall like lizards without the aid of anything but their bare hands and feet.

Next, the three of them ran to an enormous barrel filled with water and designed so that water could drain only from a spout at the bottom. David climbed up the side of the barrel, all the way to its rim, followed by the others. Keeping their distance, the boys began to run along the rim, faster and faster.

"The purpose of this drill is to walk quickly and lightly and to balance your weight against the weight of others," Grandma Wu said to me. "Now I will drain out some of the water. Over the last few months, they have been learning to balance themselves not just when the barrel is full but even when it's empty and wobbly."

I felt as if I were in a world of make-believe, surrounded by *kung fu* heroes from the fabled Shaolin Monastery and wandering warriors who had descended from Mount Liang.

"We all need to move noiselessly in times of danger and to

leave no footprints," Grandma Wu continued. "The boys also know how to leave misleading footprints. Let me show you."

Grandma Wu whistled again, and the boys leapt down from the top of the barrel. Their skin glistened with sweat, but they were not even breathing hard. I marveled at their superb physical condition and wondered if I would ever be so fit.

Grandma Wu moved to a sandy pit, which she covered with large, thin sheets of paper. One by one, the boys stepped on the paper and walked so lightly that there was not a single tear in the paper. Then she removed the paper and the boys practiced walking sideways on the sand.

"Walking sideways leaves footprints that confuse the enemy," Grandma Wu explained to me. "It's impossible to work out the direction of the footprints."

The morning continued with the boys doing a series of exercises and drills: kicking, footwork, punches, knife-hand thrusts and speed drills. Sam and Marat then rehearsed separate routines and special techniques with David in preparation for his big match the next day. I watched them rolling their bodies into balls, walking on their hands and knees like cats, tensing their stomach muscles while being pounded on their abdomens. I began to copy them, and Grandma Wu showed me a few simple movements to increase my flexibility.

The hours passed quickly, and soon it was time for lunch. Marat washed and cooked the rice, Sam whipped the eggs, David chopped the ham and I boiled pork bones in water to make soup. There was a lot of laughing and joking as we all pitched in. The boys teased me about my "clumsy hands," and I became more and more determined to catch up. I found a cookbook on the kitchen bookshelf and tried to memorize the recipes for pork-bone soup as well as fried rice with eggs and ham.

While Grandma Wu was picking herbs and vegetables in the garden, I asked the boys if they had ever had to use their *kung fu* on a secret mission.

"Our finest hour was probably that night when the three of us fought the two Russian thugs who were trying to kidnap Ivanov," Sam said, looking at Marat.

"Who's Ivanov?"

"Ivanov is my big brother," Marat said. "He is seventeen years older than me." He hesitated and looked down at the floor. "I might as well tell you everything from the beginning. Otherwise you won't get the whole picture—it's complicated."

"Russian thugs!" I said. "Are you Russian?"

"Our mother was Russian and our father was Japanese. They both died of tuberculosis when I was three years old. We used to live in Harbin, a city up north in Manchuria.

"Ivanov's best friend in Harbin was a talented French Jewish pianist called Simon Kaspe whose father owned a lot of hotels and was very rich. Times were bad. When the Japanese invaded Manchuria in 1931, some of the Russian refugees living there began to work for the Kempeitei, the Japanese secret police. The Russians would kidnap wealthy people for ransom and divide their loot with the Kempeitei. One of their victims was Simon

Kaspe. Simon's father refused to pay the ransom, and Simon was killed.

"My brother never got over it. He was determined to find the killers. He discovered that they were members of the Russian Fascist Party. But when he reported them to the French Consulate in Harbin, he didn't know that the murderers were being protected by the Japanese.

"The Kempeitei hounded him day and night. We fled to Shanghai when I was six. Ivanov enrolled me in *kung fu* classes. We became friends with Master Wu and moved next door to the academy. The Japanese left him alone for the next six years but kept an eye on him.

"About six months ago, Ivanov accompanied Sam, David and me to see a *kung fu* exhibition at the Lyceum Theater one evening. Afterward, he was on the street looking for rickshaws to take us home. The three of us were playing hide-and-seek on somebody's lawn nearby. Suddenly, we saw two rough-looking westerners jostling Ivanov. One of them took out a revolver and ordered Ivanov in Russian to raise his hands above his head. We were desperate when I happened to see a water hose that was still connected to a fire hydrant. The Russians were questioning Ivanov and not paying attention to us. I raised the hose and blasted them. Meanwhile, David sneaked up and launched a flying kick at the hand of the man holding the gun, and Sam threw a glass bottle at the other man's head. The gun flew into the air, and I caught it. I pointed the weapon at them and ordered them to lie facedown. . . ."

"Do you speak Russian as well as English and Chinese?" I asked, frightfully impressed.

"Marat and Ivanov can speak lots of languages," Sam replied proudly. "Besides the three you just mentioned, they also speak Japanese and even French!"

"As Marat was saying," David interrupted, "that was probably our most successful mission using *kung fu*. All of us could hardly believe it when the two Russians obeyed Marat and laid themselves facedown! We ran away as fast as we could and threw the gun away in a garbage can. Afterward, we discovered that we had strayed north by mistake into Japanese-occupied territory after leaving the theater. At that time, the Japanese still respected the boundaries of the International Settlement and the French Concession. They didn't bother Ivanov again until months later."

"Where is Ivanov now? Why don't you live with him?" I asked.

"I don't know where he is," Marat answered sadly. "The Kempeitei came for him in the middle of the night last December seventh and took him away. I haven't seen him since."

"December seventh again!" I said, turning to David. "Pearl Harbor Day! Isn't that the day when the Japanese killed your parents? Why does everything bad have to happen on that day?"

"Because that's the day Japan declared war on Britain and America," David replied. "Besides bombing Pearl Harbor on that day, the Japanese also took over the International Settlement of Shanghai, the part that used to belong to the British.

From then on, the Japanese could do whatever they wanted to people they didn't like throughout Shanghai. People like my parents and Ivanov."

I was thinking how sad it all was when Marat suddenly said, "The story isn't finished yet. David forgot to tell you about us going to Nan Tian Island afterward and the dolphin we befriended there!"

"That's right!" David exclaimed. "My parents were still alive then. After I got home from the Lyceum Theater and told them about the Russians, they started worrying about the Japanese coming after us. So they persuaded Grandma Wu and Ivanov to take us to Nan Tian for the rest of the summer. . . ."

At that moment, Grandma Wu walked in from the garden with fresh ginger, spinach leaves and coriander, which she washed and added to the soup. Marat's story had shaken me, but as we waited for the soup to cook, I turned to David, still full of questions.

"You were going to tell me about the dolphin at Nan Tian. How did you befriend it?"

"Marat and I went out in a boat one day," said David. "We were practicing breathing underwater with snorkels when a big dolphin swam toward us. At first, we were scared and climbed back into the boat. But instead of going away, the dolphin kept circling the boat and making clicking sounds. Then we noticed a big fishhook embedded in her body between her head and dorsal fin. A bit of fishing line was still attached.

"We didn't know what to do and were worried about sharks.

But the dolphin was asking us for help. We rowed and paddled until we reached the shore. I knew something had to be done. I found my knife and tried to calm the dolphin down by stroking her—"

"What did her skin feel like?" I asked. "I've always wanted to pet a dolphin."

"Her skin was smooth and tight, like a big wet rubber ball, and she was trembling all over. The fishhook was stuck firmly inside the muscle of her back. I just had to do it quickly, so I plunged my knife into the wound and cut into the dolphin's muscle. Once the hook was freed, I pulled it out easily.

"There was a lot of blood, so I stuffed my jacket against the wound to stop the flow, applying as much pressure as I could. I counted to a hundred, and the oozing stopped altogether."

I was entranced by the story. "Where do you keep your dolphin? Is she still there?"

"She comes and goes as she pleases," said Marat. "But David and I spent the rest of last summer playing with her. She'd appear whenever we went out on a boat, following us like a dog. We named her Ling Ling and knew it was the same dolphin because of the scar on her back. You'll have to meet her one day, CC."

"I feel useless!" I said. "All of you know so much! I've never seen a real dolphin, and don't even know how to swim! I don't think there's *anything* I can do to help the society."

Grandma Wu must have overheard because she said, "You can help, CC, in many ways. Everyone is different. David is a

51

fast thinker, Marat is a planner, Sam is intuitive. You, CC, are creative and have a love of words. Do you like to read?"

"Yes!" I exclaimed. "I love to read. How did you know?"

"Because you have a book in your hands whenever I see you. What are you reading now?"

"It's a recipe book I took from the shelf here," I said, blushing. "I want to learn how to cook."

"How about writing something for my Sunday newsletter? Don't look so surprised. We have Sunday classes at my academy every week with almost one hundred students."

"I'd love to! Oh, thank you, Grandma Wu!" I thought myself the luckiest child in the world to have been given this opportunity to write about anything I wished. I knew there were things I could express with a pen that I could never say out loud to anyone else.

After lunch, Grandma Wu announced that she was going to give us a sewing lesson. The boys rolled their eyes and groaned with dismay.

"This is as important as your *kung fu* practice!" said Grandma Wu sternly. "You need to be prepared. When you are on a mission, you will need clothes to keep you invisible." She rolled out some black material, and we spent the rest of the day sewing warrior jackets with many pockets to conceal all the items we might need, like maps, money, food and water bottles. Among the buttons she handed us to sew onto our jackets were four special ones, one for each child. These looked like ordinary buttons and resembled the others, but each was really a tiny compass.

That night, I dreamed that I was back home again. Big Aunt lived with us and everything was wonderful. I was no longer an only child but had three older brothers who played lots of games with me. As we played, I knew they cared for me just as much as I cared for them—we were a team. However, I kept losing because they were more athletic and brainy. I started to sweat because I knew I couldn't compete. Big Aunt put her arms around me and said, "Learn from your brothers and be proud of them! Brothers and sisters should be like *shou zu*, hands and feet on the same body."

I woke up in a sweat, desperate to go back to my magnificent dream. I wanted to hold on to it, but it was gone. At that moment, I missed my aunt *so* much. I wondered how she was, what she was doing and whether she was dreaming about me at the same instant when I was dreaming about her.

By nine o'clock the next morning, Grandma Wu's studio was full of children, ranging in age from seven to fourteen, with many more boys than girls. I looked around anxiously, wondering if there was anyone I knew. It would have been highly embarrassing to meet any of my schoolmates or friends. I stayed close to the three boys and sneaked glances at the children, who all looked well dressed and prosperous.

"Where do these students come from?" I asked Sam, who

was standing next to me.

"These are all fee-paying students whose parents want them to learn *kung fu* and Chinese studies on Sundays," Sam whispered. "Most of them go to missionary schools during the week, where lessons are taught in English, French or German. There used to be more students enrolled for Sunday classes, but many have moved to Chungking."

Grandma Wu organized various *kung fu* drills. Then we split into groups for calligraphy, word recognition, brush painting, history of proverbs and Confucian classics. Just before school ended, she announced that there was to be a special demonstration that day: a match between David Black and Johnny Fang, the fourteen-year-old junior boxing champion of Shanghai. David would use *kung fu* to defend himself against Johnny's fists.

We all crowded around the sand pit, where David and Johnny stood laughing and joking. The parents too. My hands were wet from sweating when Grandma Wu blew her whistle for the match to begin.

I was worried for David because Johnny was so much taller and heavier. But as in the story of David and Goliath, David stood his ground, breathing slowly and calmly through his nose. Johnny, meanwhile, paced around the pit with his mouth half open, flexing his muscles and clenching his fists.

As soon as Grandma Wu blew her whistle a second time, Johnny rushed at David like a tiger pouncing on a lamb. Just before the impact, David turned so smoothly in a circular motion that Johnny's heavy frame simply crashed onto the sand. *Wham!*

David seemed to grow taller and more luminous before our very eyes. Johnny picked himself up and charged again. No sooner did he touch David than Johnny was flipped onto the sand a second time! *Wham!* David's moves possessed a rhythm so fluid that the air itself appeared to crackle. Speed and power exploded from somewhere deep in his body, spreading themselves in sizzling waves not only over Johnny but the entire audience as well.

This must be *kung fu* in its purest form! I trembled. Every cell in my body yearned to be able to glide through the air just as David had done.

Wham! Wham! Johnny was thrown two more times. David must have touched Johnny before hurling him to the ground, but his moves were so quick that all I saw was Johnny sprawled on the sand.

A buzz went through the crowd as Johnny picked himself up.

"That was a classic demonstration of Wu Song's 'Step Back and Ride the Tiger,'" Marat murmured.

"No wonder you call him Black Whirlwind!" I asserted proudly.

David and Johnny were shaking hands to signal that the fight was over. Someone shouted, "Speech! Speech!" but David declined with a smile. Instead, Johnny stepped onto a stone bench and took the speaker-cone in his hand.

"I couldn't believe it at first and thought I'd slipped when I tried to hit David," Johnny began. "He's so much smaller than I am! But his muscles are like iron wrapped in cotton wool. A blow from him was like being shoved by a cannonball to the ground. When I tried to punch him, I kept hitting air. It was like trying to capture the wind or hit a shadow. I've never experienced anything like this before. Is he for real or is he supernatural?"

The cheering went on and on. Everyone was charmed by Johnny's generous admission of his defeat. Buoyed by the warm feelings he had generated all around, Johnny raised the cone once more. "This morning, I learned two new proverbs," he continued. "The first is *chu shen ru hua*, uncanny skill that is almost supernatural. The second is *suo xiang wu di*, irresistible force that is unconquerable. Both describe David's *kung fu* skills. I predict that he will grow up to be a great warrior! What a glorious day it will be for China when people like David finally lead us to the freedom and independence our country deserves!"

A gasp rippled through the crowd. The grown-ups looked at each other, many peering around fearfully for Japanese sympathizers. I wondered if Johnny was going to be arrested on the spot for making seditious public statements! Instead, a stout, middle-aged Chinese woman dressed in a silk *qi pao* pushed her way through the crowd and approached Johnny's bench.

"Come down at once!" she ordered sternly. "Time to go home!"

* * *

Afterward, I begged Grandma Wu to teach me *kung fu*. I told her I wanted to fight like David.

"Do you know that the words *kung fu* actually mean 'mastery of a difficult task'—any difficult task?" Grandma Wu said. "What you're really asking to learn is *wu shu*, martial arts, which has a long tradition in China, going back more than two thousand years. The martial arts we practice here at the academy were brought into China from India fourteen hundred years ago by a monk called Bodhidharma. He settled at the Shaolin Temple in Henan Province and developed a series of physical exercises to keep fit between bouts of meditation. These exercises are known as Shaolin Temple Boxing.

"Chinese martial arts are also influenced by Taoism and the forces of *yin* and *yang*. *Yin* represents female energy: that which is negative, dark and cool. *Yang* on the other hand represents male energy: that which is positive, bright and warm. The two forces regulate the universe.

"The emblem of our society is the symbol of *yin* and *yang*. Let me draw it for you. As you can see, the two fish together form a perfect circle. There is a little *yin* in every *yang* and a little *yang* in every *yin*."

"I just want to be able to defend myself, Grandma Wu," I told her.

"But first you must understand the principles underlying martial arts," Grandma Wu said firmly. "Let me tell you a story. Eight hundred years ago during the Yuan dynasty, a Taoist priest saw a bird and a snake fighting outside his window. He noticed how both animals alternated soft, yielding movements with hard, quick strikes. From these observations, he developed *tai chi*, shadow boxing. The initial movements of *tai chi* are soft and relaxed to allow you to flow with your opponent's strength until you find an opening. Then you surprise him by striking with a sudden, hard force. That was how David defeated Johnny.

"To be a *kung fu* expert, you must first be in good physical and mental health. Without basic fitness, you can't even tumble or break your fall to protect yourself, let alone launch an effective attack.

"Mentally, you must respect your teacher, pay attention during training, cultivate your patience, do your exercises conscientiously and persevere until you achieve your goal."

"How do I begin?" I asked, my head spinning.

"I'll teach you some basic moves. Promise me that you'll practice them every day. We'll work on stretching first so you can maintain your balance. Keep working at it. One day, your movements will become as fast and powerful as David's today. Only then can you claim that you know *kung fu*.

"Watch me now!" instructed Grandma Wu.

Grandma Wu went over the exercises for each day. She

showed me how to stretch, meditate and do *tai chi*. This was to be followed by one hundred fifty push-ups, side bends, sit-ups, squats, dumbbell circles and one hundred jumping jacks using a rope. Finally she said, "The whole regime will take at least two hours. We'll measure your body weekly and you'll soon develop into a true martial artist. Eventually, if you persevere, you might even become a *kung fu* expert. Now here is something that I do every morning as part of my warm-up exercises."

She lay facedown on the ground and started doing push-ups. At first, she used two hands, then one hand, then three fingers of one hand. She ended her demonstration with one hundred push-ups in rapid succession with her arms fully extended, using only her thumbs.

As I watched her with mounting respect, I remembered the proverb Johnny had used to describe David earlier. And I knew that David's *chu shen ru hua* had been inspired by her.

CHAPTER 7

Poster from Marat's Big Brother

LTHOUGH I HAD BEEN living at the academy for only three days, my life had been radically changed. So it shocked me when Grandma Wu gave me my tram fare the next morning and told me to go to school as usual. How could I go back to my old life? What if Father sent someone to the school to find me? Now I really felt like Cinderella returning to her rags after being at the ball.

But my fears were unfounded. Father didn't come to school, and my classmates didn't notice anything different about me. I sat next to my best friend, Wu Chun-mei, as usual and we played Ping-Pong at lunch break. She beat me, but the score was close and the outcome uncertain until the end. In our English class, Teacher Lin told us to write about what we liked doing best and why. I wrote about writing, how I loved it more than going on vacation, playing with dolls or anything else. When I wrote, I could be anyone I wanted to be. I could solve problems or change people's behavior any way I wished—the way I could not do in real life.

After school, it was strange to get on a different tram from the one I usually took. When I returned to the academy, I found Grandma Wu, David and Sam sitting around the kitchen table. Marat was holding a mailing tube.

I threw my bag down and joined them. Marat was trembling. "What is it?" I asked.

"Sit down, CC," said Grandma Wu. "Something miraculous has happened. You know about Ivanov, Marat's big brother? The Japanese arrested him two months ago, and we thought they might have killed him. Now this tube has arrived, addressed to me, in Ivanov's handwriting!"

I nodded, remembering what Marat had told me about Ivanov, and how the Japanese had hated him since he solved his friend Simon Kaspe's murder in Harbin.

Marat's face fell as he opened the tube. There was no letter, only a colorful poster with a picture of a large clock, its hands set to twelve o'clock. The poster proclaimed that all clocks in Japanese-occupied China must henceforth be set to Tokyo time:

WHEN IT IS TWELVE O'CLOCK IN TOKYO,
IT IS TWELVE O'CLOCK EVERYWHERE IN CHINA.
THOSE WHO DISOBEY WILL BE SEVERELY PUNISHED.

The poster was printed by the New Order of East Asia in Shanghai and had been sent on behalf of the Japanese Imperial Army.

We were speechless. Then Sam spoke up: "Why would Ivanov send us something like this?"

"The proclamation is in five languages," Marat mused, raking his fingers through his hair. "Only the top line is in Chinese. Then there are Japanese, English, French and Russian versions. Ivanov is fluent in all these languages. Maybe he's translating for the Japanese and was told to send these posters to the public. Perhaps this is his way of telling us that he's alive—"

"I have an idea," Grandma Wu interrupted. She placed the poster unrolled facedown on the table. Then she fetched an electric iron and plugged it in.

"What are you doing?" Marat asked.

"I'm waiting for the iron to get hot," she answered. "I know your brother well. Ivanov is very smart. I may be wrong, but I think he is sending us a message."

Grandma Wu held the iron above the poster without touching it. We all crowded around, feeling the radiating heat.

"Now!" Grandma Wu exclaimed. In one sudden, dramatic motion, she lifted the iron and revealed the back of the heated poster. To our astonishment, we saw line after line of neatly scripted, brownish-black Chinese characters.

"I'm sure my brother wrote this!" Marat shouted jubilantly. "I'd recognize his handwriting anywhere!"

"Fantastic!" David cried. "How did he do this?"

"Invisible ink?" Sam guessed.

"But where would he get it?" asked Marat.

"He could have used a number of things," Grandma Wu

advised. "Milk, orange juice, lemon juice, onion juice or even urine. All organic substances contain carbon, and carbon turns brownish black when it is heated. See how Ivanov used a brush when he wrote this? The pressure from the nib of a pen would have left marks on the paper. It's addressed to you, Marat! Tell us what he says."

Marat,

> *I'm risking my life by writing to you, but you've been on my mind every day since my arrest. You must destroy this as soon as you've read it.*
>
> *I'm a prisoner at Bridge House, headquarters of the Kempeitei. I have a cell to myself. The Kempeitei need my language skills. My job is to do translations seven days a week from morning till night.*
>
> *There are political prisoners here of every nationality. Normally there are twenty prisoners per cell. Men and women together. Insects and rats everywhere. It's hell on earth.*
>
> *Sometimes they make me translate confessions from Chinese, English and Russian prisoners while they're being tortured. The suffering is beyond anything you can imagine.*
>
> *The officer in charge of Bridge House is Major General Yonoshita. I've translated for him a few times. He appears to appreciate my knowledge of English because last week he told me that he wants me to teach him English.*

*I daren't write more. Don't contact me. It's too danger-
ous. My thoughts are with you. You must never forget the
kindness of Master Wu and Grandma Wu. Tell them we are
forever in their debt.* Yin shui si yuan, *when drinking
water, remember the source!*

> *Your brother,*
> *Ivanov*

None of us said a word when Marat came to the end of Ivanov's
letter. His eyes were blazing. "We have to rescue him!"

"But how?" Sam asked. "Bridge House is the stronghold of
the Kempeitei. If we try to break in, they'll simply arrest us and
put us away—"

"There are plans afoot even as we speak," Grandma Wu
interrupted him. "If we challenge the Kempeitei directly, we'll
all end up prisoners. We must find another way."

"How do we do that?" David asked.

"By putting a torch to Bridge House," Marat answered.
"Then Ivanov can come home."

"If we burn down Bridge House," Grandma Wu said
gravely, "the Kempeitei will just move to another building. To
get to the root of the problem we must destroy the *Qi* of the
men who arrested him. We have to go to the top, to the admi-
rals and generals in Japan who gave the order to bomb Pearl
Harbor. We need to fill ourselves with *Qi*. When you know in
your heart that you are right, you can fight against thousands

and even tens of thousands. But if in your heart you know you are wrong, you will stand in fear even though your opponent is the least formidable of foes."

"But how do we take away their *Qi*?" asked Sam.

"We have news from America," said Grandma Wu. "They are planning an attack on Japan and have asked us for help. Meanwhile, you must be patient. Continue your schooling and your *kung fu* practice. Becoming a *kung fu* expert will not only condition your body; it will expand your mind and give you self-confidence. Eventually, you will be brave enough to face any situation. Remember—no matter what people may steal from you in the future, they will never be able to steal your *kung fu* skills or your learning.

"As for you, Marat, your heart is aching, but at least you now know your brother is alive! Children, put your arms around Marat. Show him he is not alone!"

As we comforted Marat, I finally began to understand what it meant to belong to the Dragon Society. We were all orphans in one way or another. We, the unwanted and despised, needed each other to fight injustice. United, we would rise from the ashes and prove our worth to the world.

CHAPTER 8

Letter from Big Aunt

ARLY THE NEXT MORNING, I was awakened from a deep sleep by a mysterious sound.

Rap. Rap, I heard. *Rap. Rap. Rap.*

I opened my eyes and looked around. Where was I? I still found it hard to believe that I was no longer in Father's house.

Rap. Rap. Rap. Rap. I crawled out of bed and cautiously raised the rattan screen. Nobody there! Was it hail? But the streets were dry. Could it be one of the boys throwing pebbles at my window? Outside, it was still dark but the clock in my room said quarter past five.

I snuggled back under my quilt, but the rapping started again. This time I heard a cooing noise! Was it a ghost? I shivered and thought of hiding, but curiosity got the better of me. I crept to the window and whipped up the rattan screen as soon as I heard the next rap. There, facing me on the other side of the windowpane, was a bird with dark feathers. It had a small bill and a skin saddle between its bill and forehead. It pecked the window twice more—*rap rap*—before fluttering into the air, losing a few feathers along the way.

"Meet Da Ma, the homing pigeon, who has just flown in from Nan Tian Island," Grandma Wu said behind me.

I started—I hadn't heard her come in.

"A homing pigeon!" I declared with delight.

"Open the window and let him in. The calligraphy teacher, Miss Cheng, who had this room before, used to feed him for me. I wonder if he has brought a letter from Grandma Liu."

Da Ma settled in the room. He strutted about, bobbing his head up and down and cooing. Grandma Wu coaxed him with some seeds, cupped the bird gently between her hands and detached a metal canister attached to his leg. Inside the canister was an inner tube that contained three rolled-up sheets of paper and a key.

Grandma Wu glanced at the papers and said, "Two letters and a check! One letter for you from your aunt and one for me from Grandma Liu. This key is to your aunt's apartment."

Big Aunt's note was short and to the point.

My Precious Little Treasure,

Grandma Wu wrote and said that your father and Niang have thrown you out of their house. I was so worried until I heard that you've been staying with Grandma Wu at the academy. You'll be much safer there than at my apartment. I'm sending you my key. I have clean clothes and a spare uniform of yours in my bedroom closet. I'm also sending Grandma Wu a check.

I know it's difficult but you must write a letter of apology to your father. Tell him that you are staying at my place and going to school daily. If your father and Niang ask you to come home, then you must go back to them at once. They do not know that I have gone to Nan Tian.

Grandma Wu is a wonderful kung fu teacher and a woman of honor. Take this opportunity to learn as much as you can. You could not be in better hands.

I'm afraid Grandma Liu's leg is broken in more than one place, and it will take a long time to heal. Master Wu and I will be in Nan Tian for at least one more month. Meanwhile, study hard and take good care of yourself. I sleep more soundly knowing that you're with Grandma Wu.

Big Aunt

When I read Big Aunt's letter, so many thoughts went through my head that I could not speak. I looked up dumbly at Grandma Wu, wishing that I had the words to express myself. Immense longing for my aunt filled my whole being. Although I felt like crying, I did not want to burden Grandma Wu with yet more of my problems. So I gritted my teeth and remained silent. Then I carefully folded Big Aunt's letter and placed it with her key in my pocket.

Thankfully, Grandma Wu did not seem to notice my agitation. She was still absorbed in Grandma Liu's letter. Finally, she sighed and turned to me with a slight frown. "There is something important we want you to do for us. Your aunt has left an envelope in the safe she keeps in her bedroom closet. Since you now have the key to her apartment, you should go there as soon as it gets light. Take an empty schoolbag, pick up the envelope and your clothes and bring them back here.

"Unfortunately, it's best that you go there by yourself. It's too early in the morning for a social visit, and Japanese spies are everywhere. They will not suspect you because you are her niece and are in the habit of going there. Here is some money for a rickshaw there and back. Be very careful."

"What's in the envelope, Grandma Wu?"

"Sometimes it's better not to know." Grandma Wu sighed. "You're a child for only such a short time. . . ."

"Please tell me!" I begged. "I need to know. Telling me your secret will mean that you trust me."

"The envelope contains the contact details of our agents. We know them only by their code numbers, but their loyalty is unquestionable."

"Has my aunt been helping you?"

"I didn't know she was one of us until this very minute! Grandma Liu must have recruited her. The true identities of our agents are unknown to us. It's safer this way because there are so many traitors and double agents."

I began to understand why Grandma Wu had to be so careful. I was finding out that life for a grown-up wasn't any easier than life for a child. Maybe it was even harder. But more than ever, I wanted to be part of the Dragon Society.

Da Ma was still strutting around the room. "Do you and Grandma Liu always communicate this way?" I asked. "By carrier pigeon?"

"The postal service in Nan Tian is notoriously slow, and there are no telephones. For years we've been using pigeons to carry our mail. They are fast, reliable and discreet."

"I had no idea pigeons could carry mail!"

"Our ancestors have used pigeons for eight hundred years or more. Even the Mongolian conqueror Genghis Khan had a pigeon post system to service his enormous empire. Pigeons can also take photos! My son once designed a tiny camera out of lightweight aluminum. He attached it to the leg of a pigeon, and it photographed the terrain as the bird flew between Nan Tian and Shanghai. From these aerial photos, he mapped out the cities, mountains, rivers, roads, bridges, railroads and air-fields. But hurry now, CC, before the streets get too crowded."

I tried to creep into Big Aunt's apartment building inconspicuously, but no sooner had I put the key in the lock than I heard a familiar voice loudly calling my name. "Miss Ye Xian! Miss Ye Xian! Is that you?"

I looked around in alarm, my heart beating furiously inside my chest. Then I saw the thin, frail figure of my wet nurse, Ah Yee, hurrying up the steps to the front door. For a few seconds, I was tempted to run away. I knew she would never catch me because her feet had been bound since infancy. But as I watched her totter forth, swaying from side to side like a tree bending to the wind, I became increasingly uncertain as to what I should do.

I had known Ah Yee all my life. She came to work for us when I was less than a year old. Her own baby had died, and her husband had taken another wife. Ah Yee was the one who had nursed me when I was little, who had comforted me when Mama died, and again when Big Aunt moved out last year. More than anyone else, *she* was the one I associated in my mind with *home*. As much as I wanted to get away from her now, I stood rooted to the stone steps, moved by the concern in her voice.

She came up to me and stroked my hair. "Miss Ye Xian," she said in a trembling, tear-laden voice. "Where *have* you been? I've been worried sick."

I felt a terrible ache inside, part wistfulness and part yearning. Once upon a time, both she and Big Aunt called me *xiao bao bei*, my mother's pet name for me before she died. But one day, soon after Big Aunt moved away, Niang had summoned Ah Yee into the living room and scolded her for daring to address me so intimately.

"Who are *you*?" I overheard Niang saying to her. "Just a common maid! There are millions of peasant women who would love to have your job. My daughter is not your 'precious little treasure.' She is your boss's daughter whom you have been

71

hired to serve. From now on, you call her Miss Ye Xian, do you understand? If I ever hear you calling her 'precious little treasure' again, I will fire you on the spot. Have I made myself absolutely clear?"

Now, as I looked at Ah Yee's red-rimmed eyes and worried frown, I felt a lump in my throat. Instead of running away, I hung my head and stammered hoarsely, "Oh, Ah Yee! I—I—I don't know where to begin!"

She clung to my arm as if I would vanish. "I know you haven't been staying here. I came to look for you the night your father threw you out. Big Aunt's apartment was completely dark and no one answered the bell. Your parents expected you to come crawling home that night, begging for forgiveness. When you didn't, they assumed you were staying with your aunt. They were too angry to look for you.

"On Monday I phoned your school at three o'clock and asked to speak to you. Your teacher told me that you'd just left. I waited here for hours, but nobody came.

"I was too scared to say anything to your father, but I could hardly sleep last night. So I came here first thing this morning hoping to find you. Have you been eating properly? Tell me! Where *have* you been?"

I didn't know what to tell Ah Yee. The concern in her voice was genuine. It pierced my heart, and I could not lie. We went inside Big Aunt's apartment and sat down on the couch. The apartment was neat and silent, with the faintest fragrance of Big Aunt's lilac-scented hand lotion.

"You must trust me, Ah Yee," I said. "Big Aunt left last Friday to look after her godmother and will be away for some time. Meanwhile, I've made some wonderful new friends with whom I'm staying. Please don't look so alarmed! Everything is fine, and I'm perfectly safe. In fact, I'm doing important work that I can't talk about. Go back to my parents. Tell them I'm okay. I think we'll all be happier if I stay away from now on."

"They'll want to know where you are. So far I've told them nothing. They think you've been with your aunt all this time."

"My father was the one who told me to get out of his house!" I said angrily. "He picked me up by the back of my uniform, threw me out and slammed the door after me. What is *he* complaining of? I'm merely obeying his orders!"

"Oh, Miss Ye Xian!" Ah Yee lamented. "I was buying food at the market when your father threw you out. Otherwise I'd have died first before allowing that to happen. How could he cast out his little daughter like that? His own flesh and bone."

"Don't cry, Ah Yee," I said, squeezing her hand. "It wasn't *your* idea. Besides, I would never have met Grandma Wu if they had *not* thrown me out. Anyway, I have to go now. . . ." I wanted to pick up that envelope and get back to the academy.

"You can't leave now!" Ah Yee protested in alarm. "Where are you going? How do I know you'll be safe? What if your parents find out you're not living here? They might go to the police and report you missing. Your photo will be in the newspapers, and people will be searching for you. What a loss of face for everybody concerned! Your family will be the laughingstock of Shanghai!"

"Isn't that what they want?" I asked. "Why kick me out one day and take me back the next? Besides, I'm perfectly happy to be away from home."

"If you don't care about losing face for your parents, what about the people who took you in? Do you want to cause *them* trouble? Your niang was saying yesterday that if your aunt doesn't let you go when your father sends for you, he'll sue her for kidnapping."

Ah Yee's warning stopped me cold. The last thing I wanted was for the police to descend on Big Aunt's apartment or the Martial Arts Academy. A shudder went through me as I imagined the Kempeitei at Grandma Wu's door.

"You're right." I was thinking fast. "My friends must never come to harm because of me!"

"So the safest thing for you is to come home now, Miss Ye Xian. Tell your parents that you've been here at your aunt's apartment all this time. Eat humble pie and apologize! I'll protect you. Your father misses you, and so do I."

"No, I have a better idea. I'll write a letter of apology to my parents for you to deliver. Tell them you saw me here this morning and that I've been living here for the last four days. Don't tell them she is away. Let them think I'm with her. Niang will like it very much if you tell her that I looked terrible. The more she thinks I want to go home, the more she won't want me back."

Ah Yee wrung her hands, but I was impatient. "There's something I need to do first. Wait here. I won't be a minute."

I dashed into Big Aunt's bedroom and closed the door. Her

safe was a specially designed clothes hanger that she kept in her closet. Every time I had a good report card, she would take me into her bedroom, close the door, remove the hanger with her worn winter jacket, put the jacket on and place the hanger on her bed. Together we would turn the combination lock built into the hanger. Three turns to the right to 18. Two turns to the left to 12. Then three more turns to the right to 15.

"Open up! Magic hanger!" I would shout, and the two halves would come apart to reveal its hollow interior. She would place my report card with the others underneath her jewels, as if my grades were also precious gems impossible to replace.

I was almost in tears as I carried out our ritual by myself. This time, I had no report card. In place of my aunt, *I* was the one who wore her familiar padded jacket. It made me very homesick. The hanger opened easily. Inside, I saw her diamond watch, her jade bangle, her pearl earrings and her gold necklace. There were also a few old, faded letters, some foreign money and a small unsealed envelope that contained a list of numbers and addresses but no names. Stuck in the bottom to one side, I came across the stack of old report cards from my school.

Although I had been expecting to see them, a pang went through me. I knew I needed to leave but could not resist taking off the rubber band around the cards and flipping through them. Kindergarten—special certificate for reading one hundred books. First grade—award in creative writing. Second grade—Honors in arithmetic! Third grade . . .

Knock! Knock! I almost jumped out of my skin. Then I heard

Ah Yee's voice. "Are you almost finished, Miss Ye Xian?"

"Yes! I'm sorry!"

I picked up the envelope, shoved the cards back, closed the hanger, twisted the lock randomly a few times, rehung the jacket on top and placed it back among the row of clothes in her closet. Big Aunt's faint perfume of lilac was everywhere. Oh, Big Aunt, do you miss me too? I stuck the envelope, my clean clothes and a thick cardigan in the bag I'd brought and went into the sitting room. Ah Yee had laid out letter paper, envelope and pen for me to write to my parents.

This was what I wrote:

Dear Father and Niang,

I am very sorry that I made you unhappy last Friday. I should have told both of you that I was spending the night at Big Aunt's apartment when I phoned on Thursday afternoon. I apologize for my rudeness to you, Niang, and for biting you.

I go to school every day as usual. However, I miss Ah Yee's cooking and the comforts of home. Big Aunt has only one bedroom and I have to sleep on the floor.

Please tell Ah Yee to let me know when I can come home.

Your daughter,
Xian

I read the letter out loud to Ah Yee. She knew a few characters but had difficulty reading books or newspapers. "Don't look so worried!" I said to her. "I'm staying with Grandma Wu at the Martial Arts Academy and learning *kung fu*. The address is 2200 Avenue Pétain. Big Aunt knows where I am. She approves because I'm learning a lot. It's very important that you don't tell my parents anything!"

Ah Yee nodded but clung to my arm, still reluctant to let me go. To reassure her, I read her Big Aunt's letter. Finally, she sighed and released her hold.

"Take good care of yourself!" she said. "Ah Yee won't be there to look after you or cook what you like to eat. I always *knew* you'd grow up and leave one day. But you're only twelve years old! Are you sure you're going to be all right?"

As I let Ah Yee out of the apartment, I said to her, "I think my father wants me back, but Niang certainly doesn't. Please, Ah Yee, let me stay at the academy for as long as possible. Whatever you do, don't tell them where I am. I want to learn lots and lots of *kung fu*. Besides, I'm really, really happy there."

CHAPTER 9

Life at the
Martial Arts Academy

LL THROUGH THE RICKSHAW ride back to the academy, I was nervous and tense. In my mind, the envelope in my schoolbag took on the character of a stick of dynamite about to explode. It was after seven o'clock, and there was a lot of traffic on the streets. A truckload of Japanese soldiers in helmets rumbled by. One of them was holding a large Japanese flag, with its red rising sun against a sea of white. Farther on, I saw a policeman searching a bespectacled young man dressed in a long Chinese robe. The man stood motionless while being shoved around, holding his bicycle awkwardly with one hand. Beneath his broad-brimmed hat, his face was completely blank. I wondered what he had done to arouse the policeman's suspicion, and I began to sweat something fierce in spite of the chilly morning air. My hands were clammy, and perspiration ran from my brow.

I felt scared even though I hardly knew what I had done wrong. Was I leading a double life?

I was so relieved to reach the academy safely that I almost fell on Grandma Wu when she opened the door and helped me take my bag inside.

"Come in quickly!" she said. "I've been waiting for you. Did you find it?"

"Yes!"

"Excellent! Come with me!"

In the security of her bedroom, I handed her the envelope from Big Aunt's safe. She took a fresh piece of paper and copied a few numbers down.

"Please tell David to come here," she said. "I need him to run an errand. I have some letters to send off by pigeon post and have no time for anything else this morning."

I found David alone in his room playing his flute.

"Grandma Wu wants you," I said. "Where are the others?"

"They left a few minutes ago. Grandma Wu gave us money to buy breakfast from the street vendor today. I've been waiting for you to come back. Let's join them there after we see Grandma Wu."

Back in her bedroom, Grandma Wu handed David the paper with the code numbers she had just copied and said solemnly, "Please pass this to 0211 at once. Say nothing. Be careful!"

So just when I thought I was safe, we were back outside among the crowds, a cold wind whipping up leaves and rubbish.

I pulled my thick cardigan more firmly about my shoulders. Marat and Sam were joking with the noodle vendor on the corner.

"This guy's always here at the crack of dawn," David said to me. "When I'm up early, I see him walking past with his portable kitchen dangling from a bamboo pole perched on his shoulder."

The bamboo pole was now on the ground. A stove with a boiler on top was bubbling away at one end. At the other end was a wooden cupboard with a dozen small drawers filled to the brim with noodles, rice, flour, dumpling skins, ground pork, diced shrimp, herbs, spices, chopped vegetables, bean curd, bamboo shoots and various condiments. My stomach rumbled in anticipation.

"Five large flatbreads with deep-fried dough sticks and five cups of soya milk please," said Marat.

The noodle vendor nodded quickly and placed five sticks of twisted dough into the bubbling hot oil. The delicious smell of frying dough filled the air. He ladled hot soya milk into Marat's thermos flask, then wrapped a large flatbread around each dough stick, securing the sandwiches with toothpicks, and packed the whole lot into five large sheets of newspaper.

"There you are! Nice and hot! Fifty fen! Run home and eat your breakfast!"

"It's my treat!" David interrupted just as Marat was about to pay. David took some money out of his pocket and gave it to the noodle vendor.

While we walked away, we heard his singsong voice: "Large flatbreads! Deep-fried dough sticks! Hot soya milk!"

We were almost inside the academy when I remembered Grandma Wu's instructions. "Didn't you forget something, David?"

"What?"

"That sheet of paper for Agent 0211!"

"I know. It's done!"

"Done? I didn't see you give it to anyone!"

"Of course not! She *said* to pass the paper secretly!"

The truth finally dawned. "You mean Agent 0211 is the noodle seller?"

"That's right!"

"What's his name?"

"I don't know, and I don't want to know!" David replied.

Grandma Wu poured the steaming soya milk into bowls, and we dunked the large flatbread–dough stick sandwiches into the milk before devouring them in large bites.

"I've never had food like this before," I said between mouthfuls as the five of us sat around the table in the kitchen. "Delicious!"

"It's peasants' food, tested and true," Grandma Wu answered. "One can eat very well in Shanghai courtesy of the street hawkers. But hurry and finish now because it's almost time for school. Don't forget your *kung fu* practice and kitchen chores tonight."

I winced, as I knew her comment was directed mainly at me. Not being a natural athlete, I was finding it hard to perform even a single push-up, let alone one hundred fifty of them. After many attempts to push my body up and down a few times, I'd increased my score to twenty, but it was tough going.

The side bends, sit-ups, squats and dumbbell circles were equally exhausting. I often tripped and fell using the jump rope and found myself wheezing and gasping for breath. The first few days, my arms and legs were so stiff, I could hardly walk to the tram stop.

In spite of the pain, I stuck to Grandma Wu's prescribed routine. Six weeks passed, and finally I was able to grind out the required numbers. I gave up taking the tram. Instead, I sprinted to school and back with my schoolbag strapped to my back.

Every Sunday before classes, Grandma Wu measured our height, weight and muscle sizes. She gave each of us a notebook with a bright yellow cover to record our growth.

"In the old days, yellow was known as the imperial color because it could only be used by the emperor," Grandma Wu told us. "Nowadays anyone can wear that color because Dr. Sun Yat-sen toppled the Manchu dynasty in 1911. That's when China became a republic. Let these yellow notebooks be your own Imperial Yellow Growth Chart."

It was exhilarating to see myself becoming taller and stronger week by week. Then Grandma Wu mentioned one day that an article of mine in her Sunday newsletter had been singled out for praise by a trustee of the academy. "He asked whether CC is a pen name and wanted to congratulate the author personally," she said. "I didn't introduce you or reveal your Chinese name in case he knows your father or stepmother."

I blushed with pleasure but thanked her for being discreet. In my heart, I secretly hoped that I was changing into someone worthy of my father's respect.

Spring was in full bloom and the days grew warmer and longer. Gradually, I was included in the drills. I learned to scale the bamboo pole to the top of the wall and to run silently and swiftly. Every night, I repeated to myself what Big Aunt had said to me before she went away: "Knowledge is power. Don't let anyone drag you down. *Zi qiang bu xi*—Motivate yourself to work hard and be strong always!"

I heard nothing from my father, but Big Aunt and I sent messages regularly by pigeon post. Grandma Liu's leg was healing slowly, although she was still bed bound and unable to walk. It was a major event when Master Wu came to visit in April, bringing everyone sweaters handknitted by Big Aunt, as well as a basket of trained homing pigeons.

"How tall you've all grown!" he said when he saw us. "Especially you, CC! Look at those rosy cheeks! You're up to my shoulders now."

"I'm no longer the shortest girl in my class!" I said, beaming with pride at his compliment. "Yesterday, for the first time in my life, I won the fifty-yard dash at school. The year before I had come in last! My friend Wu Chun-mei could hardly believe it. For a change, she came in second, but she wasn't feeling well that day."

"Big Aunt will be so happy to hear this," he said. "She wants to know how your English is progressing. She misses you and asked me to take lots of photos of you."

"My English is getting better," I replied. "That's because David, Marat and Sam speak English all the time. When we speak English on the streets, it's like we're speaking a special private language. Nobody around us understands what we are talking about."

"Practice makes perfect! Language is power. You should get Marat to teach you Russian, French and Japanese as well. Knowing another language is like gaining another soul. If you knew every language in the world, you'd feel at home everywhere! What do the boys call you? CC or Ye Xian?"

"Everyone calls me CC here, including Grandma Wu!"

"See? I knew CC would suit you! It's great to see how close you've become to my mother and the boys. The five of you are like one body with four limbs! Your aunt will be so proud!"

On Master Wu's last Friday with us, the boys came home with red armbands around their sleeves, each marked with a giant letter of the alphabet. David's armband had the letter A, Sam's G and Marat's R.

"Where did *they* come from?" Grandma Wu asked, her voice unusually cold.

"Our principal, Dr. Hungate, called everyone into assembly

today," David said. "He said that the Japanese are requiring all foreigners to wear armbands. Mine has the letter A to show I'm American. Sam's is G because he is German and Marat's is R because he is Russian."

Grandma Wu and Master Wu looked at each other in dismay.

"How come nobody got armbands at *my* school?" I said.

"Probably because you're Chinese," Grandma Wu said. "You attend a Chinese school where all the students are Chinese. David, Sam and Marat go to an international school where most of the boys are foreigners. Chinese and Japanese boys are probably not required to wear armbands."

"That's right!" Sam said. "Everyone but the Chinese and Japanese boys at our school had to wear one. Dr. Hungate himself wore the letter B because he's British. Miss Van der Loot, our music teacher, wore the letter D because she is Dutch. I hate these armbands. It reminds me of the time in Berlin when my teacher forced me to pin the Star of David on my shirt. Why are the Japanese making us do this, Grandma Wu?"

"I need to find out more before I can answer you," Grandma Wu said. "Let's hold a special meeting after dinner this evening in the alcove. Meanwhile, will you children excuse us and do your *kung fu* exercises without supervision today? Master Wu and I need to talk privately."

"I wonder what's going on," Sam said as we walked to the gym to begin our exercises. "The two of them look really worried!"

"I know!" Marat replied. "Last night, I went downstairs to get a drink of water and saw them talking in the living room. It was after two a.m.!"

In the gym we paired off. Sam and Marat decided to practice the White Crane style of high kicking while David showed me the proper way of balancing myself while running on top of the barrel. I was thrilled at my progress and begged him to drain off the water, but he said I wasn't ready yet. I climbed down, and we started doing our warm-up exercises side by side.

"Are you really American?"

"I don't know what I am," David said grimly. "I told you my father was American. He was born in Chicago and worked for a British bank in Shanghai. After a few years, he got fired for going native and marrying my mother, who was Chinese. So I'm half American and half Chinese. Does that make me American?"

"That makes you American if you wish to be American!"

"If you say so," David replied. "Not many people would agree with you. I've been called all sorts of names: Eurasian, half-caste, mixed race, *za zhong* . . ."

"What does *za zhong* mean?"

"The term means 'people of mixed blood.'" David hesitated for a moment before adding bitterly, "You probably don't know this. But *za zhong* also means 'bastard' or 'son of a bitch.'"

"How awful! What about Sam and Marat?"

"All three of us 'mixed-race bastards' are here because nobody wants us, and we have nowhere else to go. Perhaps that's why we get along so well. Aside from that, getting membership here also makes us feel like we're part of something. We understand one another in so many ways. It's like we've finally found the brothers we never knew we had."

Grandma Wu walked in then and said, "David and CC, stop chatting and concentrate on your exercises! You can talk later. Please have dinner ready half an hour earlier today. Tell Sam and Marat to help you. I'm calling a special meeting at eight-thirty in the alcove tonight."

The boys and I cooked dinner while Grandma Wu and Master Wu continued to talk in private. Sam and Marat went to the garden to pick chives, ginger and scallions while David and I mixed flour with water to make dumpling skins. First we rolled the dough into long sausage shapes. Then we divided them into small lumps that we rolled until they were paper thin. From these we cut three-inch round disks.

"Tell me about your parents," I said to David as we worked.

He hesitated and went on working without saying anything.

"Don't forget I'm an orphan too," I added. "My mama died, and my papa threw me out of his house. Why were your parents killed?"

"Are you sure you want to know? It's so depressing!"

"Please tell me. I won't tell anyone!"

"Swear!"

I placed my right hand on my chest and said, "I swear. If I tell anyone, I'll be struck by lightning! Do you trust me now?"

"Yes," he said slowly. "Yes, I do trust you. I don't really like to talk about my parents. But you have a way of listening that makes me want to tell you things. Death is so final! One minute my father was defending my mother from the Japanese. The next minute he was dead."

"Why were the Japanese after your mother?"

"It all started when my parents joined the underground after the invasion five years ago. I would ride along the river on my scooter and count the number of Japanese warships docked there. We'd pass on this information to Chiang Kai-shek's secret agents.

"As you know, Chiang Kai-shek escaped to Chungking soon after the Japanese invasion. For four years, things stayed more or less the same in Shanghai. The British and the Americans were still in power in the International Settlement where we lived. But everything changed on December seventh of last year."

"The same day that Ivanov was taken away," I remembered.

"Pearl Harbor Day! The day when Japan bombed and killed two thousand Americans besides destroying eight American battleships and nearly two hundred airplanes. A few hours later on the same day, Japanese troops in Shanghai opened fire on British and American warships."

"Isn't it strange that Japan would be attacking Pearl Harbor in Honolulu and warships in Shanghai on the same day?" I asked. "Honolulu is so far from Shanghai! Honolulu is in Hawaii whereas Shanghai is in China!"

"Both attacks were part of Japan's grand plan to conquer the world and rule it with Germany. If their plan succeeds, everyone's life will be affected, including yours and mine. My dad happened to be staying at a club by the Huang-pu River that night. He was woken around four a.m. by gunfire and saw British sailors jumping from a flaming ship into the water. He ran into the street to have a better look and came across Jim Cuming, a British naval officer.

"Jim had been on shore leave and was on his way back when he saw his ship being blown up. He begged my father for help.

"I remember Dad bringing Jim home, burning the English sailor's uniform and identity papers and lending him some clothes. Then my father told me to take Jim out on the roof terrace, four doors down, to be met by Agent 0610. After a long wait in the dark, Agent 0610 finally revealed himself and took Jim away.

"When I got home people were shouting. I looked through the keyhole and saw three Japanese officers questioning my parents. They wanted to know about the British naval officer who had been spotted getting off a rickshaw outside my parents' apartment."

"That must have been terrifying," I said. "I wonder how the Japanese found out so fast?"

"I don't know. Maybe the rickshaw puller told them. The whole of Shanghai is crawling with informers.

"My parents wouldn't answer any of their questions, so the Japanese started beating my mother with a *gunto* stick. My father kicked the stick away and tried to protect my mother. One of them took out a gun and shot him in the back. They arrested my mother, and she died in jail three days later."

David's face was flushed, the memory obviously raw and painful.

"This is so terrible, David." I didn't know what else to say.

"I don't know what I would have done without Grandma Wu. She took me in, fed me, looked after me. There were days when I just wanted to die."

We were silent for a while. I tried to imagine seeing my mother beaten and my father shot before my eyes and how I would feel.

"For a long time, CC, I couldn't talk about it at all. The strange thing is . . . now that I've told you, I feel better. I don't know why, but I definitely feel better."

David added soya sauce, wine, cornstarch and sugar to a big bowl of minced pork to make filling for the dumplings.

"Were Marat and Sam already here when Grandma Wu took you in?" I asked.

"I knew them from school, but Sam has lived here since he arrived from Germany three and a half years ago. Marat and I moved here on the same day: December eighth, 1941. . . ."

"Before today I didn't know Sam came from Germany. Is he really German?"

"Well, you've seen his armband—the Japanese certainly consider him to be German!"

"What are you talking about?" asked Sam, coming in from the garden with Marat, laden with vegetables for dinner. They proceeded to wash and chop the scallion, ginger and chives.

"I wanted to know if you're German, Sam," I said, conscious

of the touchiness of my question and not wishing to offend him.

"Nationality is a tricky question." Sam's voice was bitter. "Am I German? Am I Jewish? Am I Chinese? I hardly know what I am anymore!"

There was an awkward pause. David added the chopped vegetables to the filling and sprinkled a little salt. The four of us sat around the kitchen table and began to make dumplings.

To break the silence, I asked Sam, "What's your animal sign?"

"The s-snake!" Sam said, hissing and smiling at the same time.

"That means you are a year older than I am, because I was born in the year of the horse," I noted, remembering Big Aunt's astrological chart. "Snake people are deep thinkers, full of wisdom. . . ."

"That's why Sam's nickname is the All-Knowing One!" Marat declared. "Do not underestimate Sam just because he's small. He may seem unassuming, but he's really, really brainy. Sam tops the class year after year."

"Do they really call you the All-Knowing One at school?" I inquired, greatly impressed.

"That's what they call me at the Shanghai International School," Sam replied. "But a name doesn't mean anything. Back home in Berlin, my nickname used to be *Fetus*. Same boy, different name!"

"You never told me that!" David was shocked. "Why did they call you *Fetus*?"

"Just to be mean. Sometimes they'd call me *Embryo*. I've always been small and never had much hair. For a long time, I didn't know I was Jewish. I thought I was German, just like everyone else."

"You were probably the smartest one in your class," David said. "Just as you are here in Shanghai. A lot of people are jealous of that."

"I have no idea." Sam shrugged. "It's true that I sat in the front row with all the other smart kids. Everything was fine until second grade."

"What year was that?" David asked.

"Year of the rat! 1936. Why do you ask?" Sam said.

"Because there is a Jewish boy called Stanley in my class who is also from Germany. Stanley told me his parents and grandparents were all killed by the Nazis on November ninth in 1938 because they were Jews. Stanley takes November ninth off every year and goes to the synagogue to pray."

Sam looked grim. *"Krystallnacht,"* he said. "I'll come to that later. When I was in the second grade, a teacher said in class one day that Christianity is the only true religion. I challenged her and asked about other religions like Buddhism and Judaism. Then she asked if I was Jewish.

"I told her my father was Jewish and my mother Chinese, not knowing that the answer would change my life.

"From that moment on, the teacher made me wear a Star of David on my shirt to show that I was Jewish and *different*. My best friend, Boris, would no longer play with me. If anyone spoke to me at all, it was to make fun of me. One day, I came into the classroom and Boris was sitting in my seat. He told me to get out of Germany because I didn't belong. We had a fight and everyone took Boris's side. Next day, someone pasted a copy of the anti-Jewish newspaper *Der Stürmer* on the blackboard and scrawled *Sam Eisner is a puny Jewish alien and a half-caste embryo* next to it. When I protested to our teacher, she said, 'Isn't that what you are?'"

Sam paused and looked down at his feet. I felt a tightness in my throat. Then I saw that all three boys had clenched their fists. They looked angry and sad at the same time.

"The other day, I was wondering why I like it here so much," I said, wanting to make Sam feel better. "Now I think it's because you make me feel so welcome! What Sam said just now . . . about being beaten and insulted . . . I know what it's like because that's how they treated me at home."

"The insults weren't as bad as the jokes!" Sam continued bitterly. "What I hated most was when everyone laughed at me. I remember the horrible feeling in the pit of my stomach when I'd go to school in the mornings . . . wondering what awful prank my classmates were going to pull next. Then on November ninth, 1938, the Gestapo came in the middle of the night and took Papa away. That night is called *Krystallnacht* by us Jews.

"The word *Krystallnacht* means 'night of shattered glass.' That was the night when the Nazis broke into Jewish homes and smashed the windows of Jewish stores in the cities throughout Germany. All night long, I kept hearing screams, yells and the sounds of breaking glass. I almost choked on the smoke of all the buildings burning. It was terrifying. The next morning, my mother told me we had to leave Germany for Shanghai. She said Shanghai was the only city left in the world that would accept a Jewish boy like me."

"Why did your mother say that?" I asked.

"Because Shanghai is an open city. Anyone can enter without a visa, even Jews. My mother's father had disowned her when she'd married my father, a German Jew. She knew the score! Her own father discriminated against Jews! So did the Nazis!"

"Do you know how your parents met?" I asked.

"My grandfather was a diplomat in the Chinese embassy in Berlin. My father used to go to the embassy and give my mother German lessons." Sam placed a tablespoonful of filling in the center of a disk of dough, wetted the edge with water and folded it absentmindedly into another half-moon-shaped dumpling. I looked at the rows of dumplings that we had made. They were about the same size but of four different shapes. It was as if we had signed our names across our own dumplings while making them.

"How on earth did you get to Shanghai from Berlin?" I asked.

"My mother still had her Chinese passport. She sold her jewels and bought tickets on the Italian ship *Conte Biancamano*. There were lots of Jews fleeing to Shanghai on that ship. When we finally arrived, nobody from my mother's family was there to meet us. The only person who came to the dock was Grandma Wu, who used to be my mother's private teacher when she was little. That was how I first met her. Grandma Wu took us to the academy, but then my mother got sick. The journey had taken everything out of her. She started coughing and couldn't breathe, so Grandma Wu rushed her to the hospital.

"I remember visiting her in the hospital with Grandma Wu. Even though she could hardly talk, Mama insisted that I write down the recipes of all of my favorite dishes so I could cook them myself if anything happened to her. After a while, she closed her eyes and told me that my legacy was under her pillow. Those were her last words.

"This was under her pillow."

Sam held up a piece of yellow silk. He unfolded it as we crowded around to look. His mother had used red thread to embroider a message:

You are German, Jewish and Chinese, all at the same time. You are special.

   You are in China at this moment in history for a reason. You are here to make a difference. The future belongs to you.

   Should anyone insult you or call you a za zhong, *tell yourself this: I am a child of destiny who will unite East and West and change the world.*

   Believe in yourself! Believe in your dreams! Wherever I go, I will always believe in you.

CHAPTER 10

Yi Jing: The Book of Magic

N THE ALCOVE THAT NIGHT after our dumpling dinner, Grandma Wu handed each of us a red candle in a bamboo basket. Again, she sat in the middle of the group on a stool, while Master Wu joined the four of us on the floor. She lit her own candle and turned off the lights.

"It's been some time since we held a meeting here," she began. "There have been two significant developments recently. Yesterday, there was an urgent message from our American allies requesting help on a top-secret assignment. Then today, three of you were issued armbands denoting your nationality as foreigners in Shanghai. This can only mean one thing: the Japanese are identifying all foreigners with a view of sending you to concentration camps.

"You, CC, also need to understand more about the Dragon Society of Wandering Knights. We have training centers throughout China, and our task is to select candidates suitable for membership. During the last two months, while we were teaching you *kung fu* and developing your stamina, we have also been monitoring your personality, perseverance and commitment. It normally takes at least a year of observation before a child is considered for membership.

"In your case, we have sped up the process. Matters affecting the security and future of our country need to be dealt with immediately. We are very pleased with the diligent way you have pursued your studies and the rapid progress you have made in *kung fu*. You fit in well with the people around you and have already performed valuable service on behalf of our cause. Since membership is a commitment that will affect your entire life, you should think very carefully before taking the next step. The Dragon Society requires you to take an oath of loyalty for life. Once you become a member, there is no going back."

I put up my hand.

"Please put your hand down for the time being," said Grandma Wu gently. "Remember, you may not speak until your candle is lit. Think back to the first night you were here with us. You asked me to show you how to use the book in the sandalwood box marked *Wei Lei He*, Future Vision Box. I told you then that the time was not right.

"But now the moment has come! Tonight you must seek the Yi Jing's guidance. The choice you make this evening will affect the rest of your life. *You* are the one who makes the final decision because it is *your* future. . . ."

I raised my hand again and kept it raised. This time Grandma

Wu did not object. She bent down and lit my candle with hers.

"Why am I being treated differently from the boys?"

"Because we need all four of you to carry out a vital but highly dangerous mission right away. Top security clearance is required for this task. Members only are given this privilege. All nonmembers will be sent away until our mission is accomplished."

"If you send me away, where would I go? Would I have to go back to my parents?"

"Only if you want to," she said. "Your aunt has sent us money for your expenses. One of the members of our society will be happy to look after you at your aunt's flat until she comes back from Nan Tian."

"But I like it here at the academy," I said. "I like it here better than anywhere else. Don't you want me to stay on?"

"Of course we do! That's why you've been invited to become a member. But you still need to consider carefully the disadvantages as well as the advantages before committing yourself permanently. It's only fair.

"As a nonmember, you can go anywhere you wish and live however you choose. Once you become a member, however, the society will demand total loyalty and expect you to abide by our rules. Our missions are dangerous. If they fail, you may need to hide from the Japanese until the war is over. Who knows how long that will be or even who will win? You may be arrested, tortured or worse."

"Did the boys also consult the Yi Jing before becoming

members?" I could see their faces in the dim light and felt David's gaze on me.

"Yes, of course! Every child is required to consult the Yi Jing before taking the oath."

"Thank you, Grandma Wu. Can I read the book now?"

She smiled but shook her head. "Not yet," she said. "Consulting the Yi Jing is a serious matter for which you must prepare yourself properly.

"First I must light everyone's candle."

Grandma Wu and Master Wu arranged vases of fresh flowers around the Future Vision Box on the altar table. Then they lit two sticks of incense. The candles flickered mysteriously in the scented, semidarkened room. We sat cross-legged on the floor in a semicircle, facing the altar table and the scroll with the words *Fu Dao*, Tao of Buddha.

"Let us close our eyes and meditate for twenty minutes," Grandma Wu said. "Shut out the outside world and let your thoughts go. Concentrate on breathing in and breathing out. Whisper the words Yi Jing over and over with every breath."

I did as I was told. I kept my mind free, let my thoughts go and concentrated on my breathing. Then I repeated the words Yi Jing to myself. A few minutes went by, and I began to feel calm and peaceful. I saw myself hovering in the infinite stillness of space. Suddenly a bright yellow banner appeared before me, displaying two lines of Chinese characters. Although my eyes were closed, I could read the calligraphy that was beautifully scripted in red ink:

You are in China at this moment in history for a reason.
You are here to make a difference. The future belongs to you.

As if in a dream, I heard a voice saying, "This is the end of our meditation. It's time to leave the alcove."

I opened my eyes and saw Master Wu and the boys gathering up their cushions. Grandma Wu continued, "You, CC, will now go and bathe yourself and wash your hair. Afterward, put on this robe and come back here."

She opened the lid of the Future Vision Box and took out the red robe I had seen previously. It was made of silk and had an emblem embroidered on its front and back.

"The emblem on this Taoist robe is called *Tai-ji Tu*, Diagram of the Great Ultimate," Grandma Wu said. "As you can see, it consists of two fish in a circle. One fish is black with a white dot in it. The other is white with a black dot in it. We Chinese believe that this diagram is a *Gua*, an emblem of divine guidance and wisdom.

"The history of philosophy in China began with the Yi Jing. The Yi Jing states that *yin* and *yang* are the *tao*. Therefore *yin* and *yang* are the basis of Chinese thought.

"The Yi Jing says everything in the world is divided into *yin* or *yang*. But *yin* and *yang* do not compete with one another. On the contrary, they complement and transform into each other.

100

Darkness is the same as diminished light. Light is the same as diminished darkness. *Yin* does not exist without *yang*, and *yang* does not exist without *yin*. Without night there can be no day. Without black there can be no white."

She picked up the ancient hat and said, "This Confucian Thinking Cap has six sides with the character *Jiao* printed on each side. The word *Jiao* means 'to teach.' It also means 'religion' and contains the word *Xiao*, respect for elders, within it. Education and respect for elders are the basis of Confucian thought. After you bathe, put on the hat and robe. Tie the robe with this long silk belt, which has also been embroidered with the sign of our society."

Lastly, she handed me a pair of sandals from the box and said, "On the top of each Buddhist sandal is the character *Chan*, zen, which means 'deep meditation.' Every reader should wear something Confucian, Taoist and Buddhist while consulting the Yi Jing."

After taking my bath and washing my hair, I dressed in the special garments. When I went back to the alcove, only Grandma Wu was there.

She spread a fresh clean mat on the floor for me to sit on, bowed deeply toward the altar and handed me a delicate porcelain teacup filled to the brim with tea.

"The tricolor glaze on this porcelain cup was fired during the Tang dynasty twelve hundred years ago," Grandma Wu said, sitting down next to me. "As its name suggests, the glaze consists of three colors: green, amber and yellow. The Dragon Society requires us to perform a traditional ritual known as the tea ceremony before

I can show you how to consult the Yi Jing. This teacup has no handle, and you must hold it with both hands. Shall we begin?"

I nodded.

"As teacher and pupil, we need to take alternate sips of tea from the same cup until the cup is empty. While drinking, please pay attention to the cup and its contents. The concept of mindfulness is a basic tenet of our Dragon Society. You must be aware of the consequences of your actions at all times. Please take the first sip."

The tea was delicious: I could taste jasmine, lemongrass, ginger, coriander and mint. I felt very close to Grandma Wu as we shared the tea from the same cup.

"Do you like the tea?" she asked me.

"This is the best tea I've ever tasted."

Soon enough, the cup was almost empty. Then, as I tilted the rim to savor the last few drops, I gave a scream of horror. Lying at the bottom of the cup was the distinct brown shape of a dead cockroach.

Instantly, the memory of having drunk the rest of the tea became unbearable. Pointing to the insect, I handed the cup over to Grandma Wu with my other hand and cried out, "Look at that! How disgusting!"

To my amazement, Grandma Wu received the cup with both hands and lifted it calmly to her lips, apparently still intent on finishing off the last few drops.

"I feel sick to my stomach!" I protested in a loud voice. "How can you drink that? You're going to be poisoned!"

"Poisoned? You yourself were saying just now that this was the best tea you've ever tasted. Nothing has changed. Why should I be poisoned?"

"But everything has changed! You didn't know there was a cockroach in the tea before. Now you know! So how can you go on drinking it?"

"Before you saw the cockroach, you loved the tea. As soon as you became aware of the insect, you loathed the tea instead. But the tea hasn't changed. It's *you* who have changed. It's your perception of the tea that has changed. Knowledge of the cockroach's presence has transformed your attitude completely.

"This tea ceremony was designed to point out to you the difference between perception, awareness and attitude. All of us aim to be happy. But happiness is an attitude that comes from within and is dependent on a person's perception of what is happening around her. To avoid living in a fool's paradise, one needs to perceive correctly. True perception can only come from *Wu*, mindful awareness, which develops gradually through meditation. For you to become enlightened in *Fu Dao*, the Way of Buddha, the transformation has to come from within yourself."

She raised the teacup with both hands and drank the rest of the tea as I stared at her. Then she turned the cup upside down and lifted it above her head. Surprisingly, the corpse of the cockroach did not fall out. Only when she gave me the cup to examine did I discover that the insect was made of the same tricolored porcelain and had been baked into the china.

Grandma Wu put the cup aside and handed me an expensive-looking notebook bound in black leather.

"This is a personal diary," she said. "As you see, it comes with a pen as well as a lock and key. In this book, you will write your most intimate thoughts: secrets that you don't wish to share with anybody else."

Grandma Wu approached the altar and lifted the Yi Jing deferentially out of its box with both hands. Opening its cover, she passed the book slowly through the incense smoke three times with a circular motion. I saw that the book's pages were yellow with age and covered with mysterious symbols. Along the margins and between the lines were numerous handwritten notes.

Grandma Wu untied the knot around the bundle of sticks protruding from the pouch next to the Yi Jing's spine and said, "You will get out of the Yi Jing what you put into it. For thousands of years, we Chinese have considered this to be a book of magic and have treated it with reverence. I will be leaving in a few minutes. When you are alone, cleanse your mind of every distraction and concentrate on what you wish to ask the Yi Jing. Unlock the notebook I just gave you and write your question there. Take your time and don't rush. Remember to leave space on the same page for the Yi Jing's answer.

"Then take the yarrow stalks from the pouch and start dividing them. Let me show you how. Our ancestors believed that the yarrow plant represents the spirit of Nature and considered stalks from this plant to be particularly suitable for divination purposes.

"While dividing the stalks, be constantly aware of the question you have written to ask the Yi Jing. Think of it all the time.

When you have finished dividing the stalks, you will end up with a number between one and sixty-four.

"There are sixty-four *Guas* in the Yi Jing. Each *Gua* is a separate emblem of divine guidance and wisdom. Between them, the sixty-four *Guas* contain the answer to every situation that might arise. There is a chart at the end of the Yi Jing. Consult this chart after you receive your numbered *Gua* from dividing the stalks. Turn to the page corresponding to the *Gua* you have been given. Read its meaning and significance. Copy it down in your black notebook below your original question on the same page. This is the Yi Jing's answer to your question."

She handed me the Yi Jing, and I received it with trembling hands.

"You will see that each *Gua* is a symbol made of six parallel horizontal lines, one on top of another. Some lines are divided in the middle. Others are whole. Think of them as seeds containing all the answers to every question in the universe."

Gua Number 1:
Heaven

Gua Number 2:
Earth

"How is it possible," I asked doubtfully, "that a bunch of divided and undivided lines can represent everything in the universe?"

"A German philosopher named Leibniz who lived in the seventeenth century thought this possible. While reading the Yi Jing, he came up with the idea of a new number system and called it binary mathematics. He thought of each divided line as *zero* or *yin*, and each undivided line as *one* or *yang*. He wrote that every situation in the universe can be represented by using only the numbers zero and one. My son, Master Wu, tells me that American and British scientists are developing a miraculous new machine called a computer based on Leibniz's theories.

"But now let me show you the proper way of dividing the yarrow stalks. Then I'll leave you alone."

Grandma Wu showed me how to start with fifty stalks and to place one stalk in a prominent place on the altar. This was to be the observer stalk representing Heaven or a person's conscience. "Even though we may think we are alone," she said, "our conscience is with us at all times. When you've finished, always thank the observer stalk for its participation."

As soon as Grandma Wu left the alcove, I got up and placed the Yi Jing back in its box on the altar table. I went to my cushion, unlocked my black leather diary, inscribed the date and time on the first page and began to write:

> *I am going to confide everything to you, including my feelings about my father, Niang and Big Aunt. In return, I hope you will give me comfort and consolation.*

I closed my eyes and thought of my aunt, wondering whether she would be proud of me for being invited to join the Dragon Society of Wandering Knights. A pang went through me when I thought of the English lessons at her flat and the delicious snacks she used to make every afternoon, just for the two of us. Then I remembered my stepmother and the sensation of Niang's sharp fingernails digging into my throat. This was followed by the memory of my father lifting me by the back of my uniform and throwing me into the street. Last of all, I thought of my companions at the academy: Grandma Wu with her wisdom and understanding; Master Wu with his skills and intelligence; and the three boys. Beneath their carefree exteriors, how they had all suffered! Marat with his brother, Ivanov, in jail; David witnessing his parents' murder; and Sam being vilified and expelled from his own country. By becoming a member, would I recover the family I lost when my mother died and my aunt went away?

The yellow silk banner appeared again in front of my closed eyes, and I saw the final message left by Sam's mother: *You are in China at this moment in history for a reason. You are here to make a difference. The future belongs to you.*

I turned to the second page of my diary and slowly wrote my question:

> *I would like to join the Dragon Society, but I don't want to leave my aunt. I can't live with my stepmother, but I'd like to see my father again. I want my aunt and my father to be proud of me. Should I take the oath and become a member?*

I placed one yarrow stalk in front of the Future Vision Box, then took the other forty-nine into my hands and divided them the way Grandma Wu had done, thinking of my question the whole time. During the forty-five minutes it took to arrive at the number of my *Gua*, I tried to visualize the faces of Big Aunt, my stepmother and my father. I thought of leaving home permanently, becoming an expert in *kung fu* and accompanying Grandma Wu and the three boys on their missions throughout China. Would my aunt and father be proud of me then? What if I was arrested? Would I cause trouble for my relatives?

Eventually, I arrived at the final number. The answer to my question was *Gua* number 13. I took the Yi Jing from its box and turned to the last page. There I found the page on which was printed the meaning of *Gua* number 13.

 Gua Number 13: Fellowship with Like-minded People

With mounting excitement, I copied the Yi Jing's comments in the space I had reserved for it.

Gua *number 13 (*Tong Ren*). Like-minded people are gathered together to be trained. Surroundings are dangerous and wild. Nevertheless, it is favorable for you to join with the others and undertake this worthy endeavor.*

I felt the hair rising at the back of my neck as I read and reread the Yi Jing's answer to my question. It was clear and definite. The Yi Jing was advising me to take the oath, join my friends and become a member of the Dragon Society.

I thanked the observer yarrow stalk and bowed three times to the scroll marked *Tao of Buddha* hanging behind the altar. Then I stashed all the yarrow stalks back in the Yi Jing's pouch. I changed into my normal clothes, blew out the candles and went back to my room with my black diary.

Grandma Wu was waiting for me there. She smiled. "What have you decided?"

"I would like to join."

"No doubts at all?"

"None whatsoever!"

"Good! It's getting late. But before you go to sleep, I want to tell you something. Do you remember the day we first met?"

"At your bookstall in the bazaar behind the park? Of course I do."

"If you had come to the stall one day later, we would not have met."

"What a coincidence! How is that so?" I asked.

"Members take turns staffing the society's businesses around the city. After twelve months, my term of duty at the bookstall was over. The bookseller who replaced me is Grandma Wang, an accomplished artist. The day we met was my last day there."

"How lucky I am! One day later and my life would have been different!"

"That's called fate, CC," said Grandma Wu, "and there is nothing you can do about it. However, consulting the Yi Jing is a different matter entirely. Can you tell the difference now?"

"Yes! When I consulted the Yi Jing, I had the opportunity to make my own choice and decide my own future."

"That's right! Have a good night's sleep. Tomorrow is Saturday. There is no school, but I have called a meeting at seven sharp."

She did not ask and I did not tell what had transpired between the Yi Jing and me.

CHAPTER 11

The Password

EXT MORNING, AFTER A quick breakfast of steamed bread and soya milk, Grandma Wu called a meeting around the kitchen table.

"I wish to congratulate CC on becoming the newest member of our Dragon Society," Grandma Wu began. The boys clapped and cheered while Master Wu leaned across the table to shake my hand. "All four of you have suffered through no fault of your own. CC has been thrown out by her father, and you three boys have been orphaned by the war.

"Unfortunately, there is a lot of prejudice in Shanghai against Eurasians and orphan girls. But should any of you encounter hostility or rejection, seize that negative energy you feel coursing through your veins and use it for a positive goal. Prove to the world that you are worthy of respect. Don't mess up your lives by being bitter and self-destructive!

"From now on, the six of us will belong to the same family.

No one needs to be alone again. You four children have been chosen to be part of an elite corps of secret agents embarking on a daring mission. One by one, please place your left hand on top of mine with your palm facing downward. You first, Master Wu, followed by David. Since David is the oldest among the four of you he will be your *Da Ge*—Big Brother. Place your hand on top of David's, Sam. You are *Er Ge*—Second Older Brother. Your hand above Sam's, Marat, as *San Ge*—Third Older Brother. CC's hand goes on the very top. Being the youngest, she is everyone's *Xiao Mei*—Little Sister.

"Let's now squeeze our left hands together to make a giant fist! In unity there is strength. At the same time, place your right hand against your heart and repeat after me:

"I swear to be loyal and true to the Dragon Society and to my fellow members, with whom I am united from now until the end of my life.

"I promise to practice mindfulness, awareness and true perception through meditation daily.

"I will turn negative emotions into positive Qi *and achieve great deeds by following the Tao of Buddha at all times."*

As I repeated the words after her, I thought how radically my life had changed. Under Grandma Wu's guidance, my future was now full of hope. I closed my eyes and made a silent promise to her that I would always try my best to be mentally alert, morally upright and physically strong.

"This ends CC's initiation ceremony," Grandma Wu said. "Congratulations!"

"You did it! You did it!" Sam cheered.

"You may not realize it at this stage of your young lives," Master Wu said, "but one of the most difficult things to find in life is true friendship. Now that the four of you have the opportunity to become close, you should do so. As the years go by, little friends will grow up to be great friends.

"But now that we have sworn the oath, we need to tackle the task at hand. The Americans have asked us for help. At this very moment in Hawaii, sixteen B-25 bombers are being loaded into an aircraft carrier, the USS *Hornet*. Each plane has a crew of five, so there will be eighty American airmen altogether. When the USS *Hornet* is four hundred and fifty miles from Japan, the planes will take off from the ship and fly toward Tokyo. When they have completed their raid, the pilots will refuel their planes in eastern China.

"Chuchow in Zhejiang province is only one hundred miles inland from China's coast. That's where the Americans will refuel. Afterward, they will fly west to Chungking and then on to India via Burma on their way home. Our help is needed in Chuchow."

"When will they bomb Tokyo?" Marat asked, his eyes shining. I knew that he was thinking of his brother, Ivanov, locked up under Japanese guard in Bridge House. Since the letter written in invisible ink on the back of the poster, Marat had heard nothing from him.

"The USS *Hornet* is scheduled to leave Hawaii tomorrow, the twelfth. It will take the ship about six days to cross the Pacific Ocean. They plan to launch the planes on the evening of April eighteenth and reach their targets in the dark of night, to avoid Japanese antiaircraft fire. Hopefully, they'll land in Chuchow on the morning of the nineteenth."

"Why don't they land on the Chinese coast? Wouldn't that be closer to Tokyo?" David asked.

"China's coastline is in Japanese hands," Grandma Wu answered. "It's true that Chiang Kai-shek's troops are in control of Chuchow, but the Japanese army is not far away. In addition, the Japanese are using Chinese puppet troops under the collaborator Wang Ching-wei to patrol that area. But I believe the hearts of many of Wang's soldiers really belong to China. They may be willing to assist the American pilots in secret."

"How can we help?" Sam asked.

"We have been training you for exactly this type of task," Grandma Wu disclosed. "Because you all speak fluent Chinese and English, your help will be essential when the Americans land in Chuchow. The pilots probably won't be able to tell a Japanese from a Chinese."

"Except one is an enemy and the other is a friend!" Sam added.

"That's right," Master Wu agreed. "Sometimes we have difficulty telling the difference between enemies and friends ourselves. Grandma Wu is using passwords to determine who is on our side."

"The passwords come from our history," Grandma Wu announced. "Twenty-two hundred years ago, China was divided into warring states, and the King of Chu had been killed by the King of Qin. The people of Chu mourned the loss of their king and made the following vow: *Chu sui san hu, wang Qin bi Chu*— even if there are but three families left in Chu, the Qin empire will be toppled by a native son of Chu. Over the years, this saying has become a proverb symbolizing the undying *Qi* of a conquered nation. It is the code for our mission."

"Secret agents will identify themselves by uttering the first half of the couplet, *Chu sui san hu*, twice," Master Wu said. "You will respond by repeating *wang Qin bi Chu* four times in rapid succession. Repeating this phrase will replenish your *Qi* and strengthen your determination."

"In the case of a dire emergency where action needs to be taken immediately, you will give warning by repeating the first half of the couplet, *Chu sui san hu*, four times in rapid succession," continued Grandma Wu, "You will dress and behave like local peasant children. Here are four cone-shaped bamboo hats, the black warrior jackets you tailored for yourselves, four pairs of cotton trousers and four pairs of straw sandals. It's important for you to blend in with the crowd and not be noticed."

"But these trousers look like they've been worn by someone else before!" Marat complained. "In fact, there is a hole in the knee of mine!"

"Come on!" David exclaimed indignantly. "We're not going to a fancy-dress party! This is a mission to save the lives of

American pilots! Do you want to save lives or look nice?"

"Sorry," Marat mumbled. "You're right!"

"Since you'll resemble local peasant children when dressed in these clothes, the Japanese are unlikely to bother you," Grandma Wu said. "Keep your eyes and ears open at all times. You will be staying with secret resistance fighters, but spies are everywhere and the Japanese are powerful. When the time comes, I'll be phoning your teachers to excuse you from school."

She handed each of us a small box containing a battery-operated radio transmitter through which we could receive and send shortwave radio signals. "I'll teach you how to intercept and decode radio messages," she said. "Let's spend some time practicing. These are the secret codes. By dialing into the following radio frequencies, you'll be able to hear coded messages being transmitted by the U.S. as well as the Japanese navy. Marat, I'm appointing you as our chief radio operator on this mission because you're fluent in Japanese."

"Who's the American leader of the raid?" David asked.

"Colonel Jimmy Doolittle."

"Doolittle?" David said. "I've heard of him. Isn't he the one who holds all those flight records? For speed, endurance, distance and altitude combined?"

"That's right! He is one of the volunteer airmen on this mission. We have to hope that the U.S. aircraft carriers aren't spotted by the picket boats patrolling Japanese waters," warned Master Wu. "You children must listen very carefully for radio signals and decode them as fast as possible. We need to warn our

American allies at once if their carriers are spotted by the Japanese."

"When are we leaving?" Marat wanted to know. "There are only eight days left before the pilots are due to land in Chuchow. Today is already the eleventh."

"Master Wu will be leaving today to orchestrate arrangements in Chuchow, but we still have a few days before Saturday the eighteenth," Grandma Wu replied. "Say nothing to anyone. Start getting your things ready. Put on your peasant clothes instead of your school uniform when you get up on Friday. We depart first thing that morning."

CHAPTER 12

The Mission

E SET OFF BY TRAIN at first light on Friday, April 17, accompanied only by Grandma Wu. During the journey from Shanghai to Chuchow, we were given a private compartment by a trusted train attendant. As soon as the train left the station, the attendant closed the curtains and locked the door of our chamber, giving us total privacy. "I have checked," he said. "You are safe. No Japanese aboard."

"Who is he?" I asked when we were alone.

"I only know him as Agent 0108," Grandma Wu said. "It's better not to know his true name or anything about him in case we're questioned by the Japanese."

From time to time, one of us would part the curtain to peek at the terrain we were traveling through. Outside, it started to rain. The countryside was relatively flat, and all we could see through the mist was endless rice paddies. Here and there we saw men and oxen pulling primitive-looking wooden ploughs to till the fields. Every inch of land appeared to be cultivated. From time to time, we passed clusters of houses in the distance that looked like villages.

We left our compartment only when absolutely necessary and avoided talking with anyone. Most of the people on the train seemed to be farmers and small businessmen. There were a few women traveling with their children. Thankfully, we did not come across any Japanese soldiers. Whenever the train stopped at a station, swarms of peddlers would approach and try to sell passengers their local produce, handicrafts and foodstuffs.

The train pulled into Chuchow later that afternoon. The town was surrounded by a wall and crisscrossed by cramped streets filled with pedestrians, wheelbarrows, rickshaws, pedicabs and bicycles. We saw no trams, but there were a few buses and motorcars. Outdoor stalls occupied every nook and corner of the large square surrounding the train station. Grandma Wu led us to a noodle vendor and bought each of us a bowl of steaming hot noodles topped with bean curd sauce. She handed us chopsticks, and we ate standing up. While we were eating, a hot-water seller in the next row of stalls asked me in a loud voice, "Little Sister! Would you like to buy a nice cup of freshly boiled water to drink?" I shook my head just as he pointed to a sweet-gruel seller who was beckoning me with his hand. As David and I approached, he murmured something.

"Excuse me," David said. "We didn't hear you. What did you say?"

This time the sweet-gruel seller answered in a distinct

voice, "*Chu sui san hu, Chu sui san hu.*"

David and I looked at each other dubiously. Was this gruel seller in baggy trousers, dirty apron and cloth shoes our contact man in Chuchow? But there was no doubt what he had just said. And he had said it twice. Then I heard David take a deep breath and say, "*Wang Qin bi Chu,*" four times in rapid succession.

The man's response was immediate. "Come with me!" he said. He unpinned his apron and said something to a woman behind him. With mounting excitement, we called Grandma Wu, Sam and Marat and followed the gruel seller out of the square.

"I am Agent 0220," he told Grandma Wu. "I had no trouble spotting the five of you but needed to make sure. Please follow me. Everything has been arranged. We are going to a safe house that belongs to an American missionary. You will have the house to yourselves."

We arrived at a little stone house situated close to the city wall at the edge of town. Our guide was a quiet man who said nothing to us along the way. When we reached our destination, he simply unlocked the dark red, double-leafed front door, handed us the keys and bade us good-bye.

We stepped into a tidy but plainly furnished living room with a long couch, wooden floors and curtained windows. The house had only one bedroom with a large double bed and mats on the floor. That night, all five of us shared the same room. Grandma Wu slept on the bed while we children slept on cushions from the couch spread out on the floor.

Grandma Wu woke us before dawn for a quick breakfast of

hot rice congee and salted duck eggs, which she had found in the kitchen. As we ate, the rain kept falling outside.

"Let's get to work," decreed Grandma Wu. "It is now precisely five-oh-two a.m., Tokyo time. Let's synchronize our watches. Adjust your listening devices and shortwave radios. If you hear a signal, decode it straightaway. Record the time and date of each message."

Just after 6:30 A.M., Marat intercepted a radio message from a Japanese ship in the Pacific Ocean off the coast of Japan.

"Grandma Wu! Grandma Wu!" he called urgently. "I just heard someone identifying himself as the radio signalman from the *Nitto Maru* sending this message in Japanese: 'Three U.S. carriers sighted seven hundred nautical miles east of Tokyo at six-thirty a.m. Tokyo time.' Is the *Nitto Maru* one of those Japanese picket boats?"

"Alert the Americans at once," cried Grandma Wu. "This is important and serious!"

Marat nodded solemnly. The rest of us listened intently.

Almost immediately after Marat had transmitted his message to the Americans, I heard the USS *Hornet*'s radio operator ordering two American ships, *Nashville* and *Enterprise*, to bombard and sink the *Nitto Maru*.

All at once, the enormity of what we were involved in hit me, and I started to tremble uncontrollably. It was no longer a game. The stakes were immense. This was war, with its million horrors.

"What about the sailors on the *Nitto Maru*?" I asked. "Are they going to die?"

"There is no alternative," Grandma Wu lamented. "Either we destroy them or they destroy us. This is the price we pay for China to regain her independence."

I thought of the men at sea losing their lives, drowning in the burning flames; the sailors on both sides being torn to bloody shreds; the moans of the wounded; the grief of the widows and the plight of their fatherless children at home. Was war truly the only answer?

"The Japanese are still dispatching messages to the *Nitto Maru*," Marat cried. "They don't know that it's been sunk, but they must suspect something. I just heard Admiral Matome Ugaki issuing an emergency order to repel a major enemy fleet off the Japanese coast. Japanese airplanes, destroyers, cruisers and submarines are heading toward the position last reported by the *Nitto Maru*. The Americans should launch their planes right away, so their carriers can make a quick getaway. Otherwise the Japanese will destroy them."

"Children! Radio the *Hornet* immediately and report what you have just heard!" commanded Grandma Wu. "Otherwise, all will be lost!"

"But the American ships are still so far from Japan!" Sam objected. "Master Wu said the planes were supposed to take off when the *Hornet* is four hundred fifty miles away from the Japanese coast. They are still seven hundred miles away. They'll run out of fuel for sure!"

The original plan was for the planes to take off just before sunset and bomb Japan under cover of darkness. Now they would be arriving in Tokyo around noon, in full sight of Japanese anti-aircraft guns. The earlier takeoff and increased distance to Tokyo meant that the American pilots would be flying to Chuchow with empty fuel tanks. We hated to admit it, but Jimmy Doolittle's raid on Tokyo was turning into a suicide mission.

For a while we were all silent, thinking of what the American pilots must be going through. What choice did they have? If they aborted the raid, they risked the loss of their aircraft carriers as well as their planes. If they went ahead, they risked flying with empty gas tanks over the open sea. Every decision was riddled with danger.

"If I were one of Jimmy Doolittle's pilots, I'd volunteer to take off right now," announced David, his face flushed. "Do or die!"

"So would I!" agreed Marat fervently.

"Me too!" concurred Sam.

I could hardly speak but knew that I would also risk my life.

"Admiral Halsey, the task force commander, agrees with you," Grandma Wu declared, her transmitter clamped to her ears. "The admiral just ordered Colonel Doolittle to launch the planes immediately. As we speak, sixteen brave American pilots and their crews are setting off on the bombing raid."

CHAPTER 13

Chuchow Airfields

 **E KEPT OUR EARS** glued to the radio transmitters for the rest of the morning, but there was no further news. Early in the afternoon, there was a persistent rapping on the door. When I looked through the peephole, I saw a young man wearing a white doctor's coat and thick glasses.

"I'm looking for Grandma Wu," he said breathlessly.

"What's your name?"

He placed his right hand against his heart, clenched it into a fist and said, *"Chu sui san hu! Chu sui san hu!"*

I remembered the response we'd been taught and repeated it four times before calling for Grandma Wu and welcoming the man into the house.

"I'm Dr. Chen, physician and head of the local resistance in Chuchow and Linhai," the man told us. "I have terrible news. So far, no fuel or flares have been delivered to the Chuchow air-

124

fields. The radiomen sent by Chiang Kai-shek to operate the homing radios at the airfield have not arrived because of bad weather. Unfortunately, the forecast calls for more rain and heavy fog this evening. Visibility will be limited to a hundred feet or less.

"The American pilots were told there would be homing signals and flares to mark the runways of Chuchow airfields. Now there will be nothing to guide them. And no fuel is available even if they do land successfully. These pilots are doomed! What should we do?"

Grandma Wu was gripping her chair. She closed her eyes and covered her face with her hands for a few minutes.

Then she took a map out of her pocket and scrutinized it for a long time. When she looked up, her voice was resolute. "Although we have no fuel for the American planes, we do have four capable and multilingual children who are eager to help the crew. It is clear from this map that the pilots will have to make some difficult choices. When they run out of fuel, they'll need to abandon their planes and parachute out. The question is, If they can't make it to Chuchow, where will they end up and how can we help them?

"The planes should have enough fuel to cross the East China Sea. If they manage to get at least seventy miles inland from the coast, they will have a chance. But if they don't make it that far, the planes will either crash into the ocean or land on one of the beaches. It is possible that the survivors will land on the coast, or even on Nan Tian Island itself.

"I suggest we go straight to Nan Tian. I have seen aerial photos of the island taken by my pigeons. Nan Tian has a long flat beach that is not only visible from the air but also suitable for emergency landings. It will be risky for the Americans as the island is under Japanese control, but we have many contacts there and know the man in charge of the local guerrillas. They will help us."

My heart leapt! Big Aunt was at Nan Tian Island. Perhaps I would see her again.

Grandma Wu turned to Dr. Chen and said, "I'll write a note to Agent 0958 and inform him that we will be arriving in Nan Tian this evening. Please send it off by pigeon post immediately. Let's keep in touch the same way."

"They've done it! They've done it!" Marat shouted at this moment from the other side of the room. His face was ashen, but his voice exhilarated. "I've just heard an announcement from Tokyo radio JOAK that American bombs have fallen on four Japanese cities this afternoon. This is the first time in the history of Japan that any of her cities was ever invaded by an enemy. To add insult to injury, not a single American plane was shot down."

"Hooray for Jimmy Doolittle and his pilots!" heralded Grandma Wu. "The Americans have taken away the enemy's *Qi*. Japan is no longer invincible. Jimmy Doolittle has brought the war home to Tokyo. Let us hurry now to Nan Tian Island in case one of the American planes should crash-land there. The crew will be needing us!"

CHAPTER 14

Nan Tian Island

ATER THAT SAME evening, two fishermen met our boat at the dock on Nan Tian Island. They shepherded us into a quaint, thatched-roof hut at the head of a long, curving bay. David whispered that the fishermen must be members of the local underground. Although I was dying to find out whether the two men had been sent by Master Wu, Big Aunt or Grandma Liu, I dared not ask.

It was foggy, cold and wet, and the wind was biting. We could hardly see anything in front of us. No one mentioned it, but all of us knew that the American pilots would have a terrible time landing anywhere in this weather.

Grandma Wu built a fire with straw and charcoal. She made soup noodles with salted fish brought to us by the fishermen. We wolfed it down. Afterward, we huddled around the warm stove with our radio transmitters clamped to our ears, hoping to intercept signals from the pilots, but we heard nothing.

Marat, who was fastidious about cleanliness, insisted on giving himself a cold sponge bath even though he had to get water from the well outside. The rest of us sat on the floor fiddling with the radio knobs, bent on listening. Despite our best efforts, Marat was the only one who successfully decoded any more messages. As soon as he rejoined us, he reported that Japanese naval units were swarming into the East China Sea in search of U.S. aircraft carriers and abandoned planes. He also located a radio station from Chungking that declared that the people on the streets there were celebrating Doolittle's successful raid. Chiang Kai-shek's war minister announced that the "nightmare of Japan's invasion of China has been shattered by American bombs. The Americans will soon bring justice and freedom to us Chinese people."

Suddenly, we heard an insistent pounding on the door. Grandma Wu sprang up to see who it was. A guttural male voice repeated the password, and Grandma Wu responded, opening the door. A fisherman stood there dripping, dressed in a raincoat made of palm fibers and wearing straw sandals. He closed the door carefully and stared at us.

"So many children . . ." he began hesitantly.

"*Wang Qin bi Chu!*" Grandma Wu interrupted, holding her hand over her heart and making a fist. "Speak freely! You can trust these children."

"My name is Li Cha," said the fisherman, "and I am the leader of the Nan Tian guerrillas. An American airplane has just crashed near the beach half a mile away. There are five crew members on board. They are alive, but four are injured."

"Where are the Japanese?" asked Grandma Wu.

Li Cha looked around fearfully. "There are no Japanese troops on this island at the moment. But their boats patrol the area. They are bound to spot the American plane wreckage sooner or later. We need to put the airmen on a boat and sail for the mainland as soon as possible."

"Then we have no time to waste!" Grandma Wu decided. "Children! Go with Li Cha at once and bring the Americans here for the night. I have some herbs in my bag that will provide pain relief if they are hurt. I'll stay here and prepare for them."

The four of us rushed out in the highest excitement with Li Cha into the pouring rain and made our way along the beach. It was pitch-black outside with neither moon nor stars to guide us. Li Cha led the way, holding a small flashlight, with us following behind in a single file. At first, I saw nothing and heard only the booms, hisses and roars of waves waxing and waning against the sand. We rounded some rocks, and I could now make out the shapes of five tall figures sprawled on the seashore, lit grotesquely by the flickering flames of their burning plane. A pungent odor of spilled gasoline and burning metal permeated the air. As we approached, one of the airmen struggled to his feet, clutching a pistol fearfully.

David shouted in English, "We're Chinese. My friends and I can speak English and Chinese. We are here to help you."

"You don't know how wonderful it is to hear you say that!" The soldier put away his weapon and came forward. "I am

David Thatcher. Where are we? Are we in Chinese- or Japanese-occupied territory? We desperately need a hospital!"

"You must come with us," said David. "You've landed on Nan Tian Island, which is controlled by the Japanese. There are no hospitals here, but we can help you. Are there any more airmen in the plane?"

Thatcher shook his head. "There are no others. All five of us escaped when our plane crashed into the sea. Ted here has the worst injuries." He bent over a groaning man and continued to bandage his bloody leg with a strip of dirty fabric. As Li Cha shone his flashlight on one flier and then the next, David Thatcher quickly introduced them.

All the men were in great pain, but the pilot, Ted Lawson, seemed to have suffered the worst injury. He had lost many of his teeth. His face was bruised and filthy. A gash on his leg was so deep that I could see the bone beneath the muscle and gristle. Charles McClure, the navigator, had dislocated both of his shoulders. They were swollen down to his elbows, and he could hardly move his fingers. Robert Clever, the bombadier, had blood around his eyes and on top of his head. Dean Davenport, the copilot, had cut his lower leg but could still walk.

Li Cha had been standing back, but now he whistled sharply, and eight other men appeared from the shadows. Together we helped the Americans limp back to the hut.

Grandma Wu placed Lawson on the only bed in the outer room, covered him with a quilt and gave each American a bowl of the hot herbal soup she had brewed. While we tended to the injured airmen, Marat and Sam accompanied Thatcher back to the beach to salvage first aid supplies from the airplane.

They came back soaking wet. The plane had broken into several pieces and incinerated on impact. Now only the tail was left sticking up from the sand. Instead of bandages, morphine and iodine, they had only managed to find a carton of cigarettes. David tore off the cellophane and lit one for Lawson, who seemed more comfortable now that he had drunk the warm bowl of medicinal soup. He inhaled deeply with satisfaction.

"Hey, kids! What are your names?" Lawson asked.

There were introductions all around. But when it came to Li Cha, Lawson kept forgetting his name.

Finally Sam suggested, "Li Cha's surname is Li, and his given name is Cha, which means 'tea' in Chinese. In China, the surname comes before the given name. Why don't you call him Cha Li, or Charlie? This way you'll remember."

"Great idea!" Lawson said. "I'll call him Charlie from now on."

Li Cha turned to Sam and said, "Tell the Americans I'm leaving now to arrange for a boat to take them to the mainland first thing tomorrow morning. I'll be back at dawn. Meanwhile, you should all get some rest. Tomorrow will be tough."

Grandma Wu nodded. She was exhausted. But the three boys and I were much too excited. We decided to stay up and keep the airmen company.

Lawson, Davenport, McClure and Thatcher sat on the bed with their backs against the wall. Robert Clever lay quietly in an opposite corner and appeared to have fallen asleep. The boys and I squatted on a mat next to the airmen while they smoked their cigarettes and sipped cups of hot water.

Lawson was not used to drinking hot water. His injuries were severe, and he had lost a lot of blood. He kept saying he was thirsty. I volunteered to keep up his supply of hot water, but he begged for cold water.

"It's not safe to drink cold water in China," Sam informed him firmly. "My mother said I must only drink water that has been freshly boiled. We call boiled water *kai shui*, opened water, or *gun shui*, rolling water. Water 'opens' and 'begins to roll' when it comes to a boil. Only then is it safe to drink. Cold water is full of germs and will give you all sorts of diseases."

"Tell you what," I proposed. "I'll boil a pot of water and keep it in bowls until it cools. That sort of cold boiled water will be safe for you to drink."

"Thanks, kid!" Lawson said. "Let me give you something. Here are three American coins, one for each of you boys. CC, you can have my pilot's badge as a souvenir. Let this be a symbol of friendship between America and China. Pass this over to your girlfriend, will you, Sam?" He unpinned the flying wings from his shirt and handed the badge to Sam.

"She's *not* his girlfriend," David objected in an irritated voice.

"I am no one's girlfriend," I said, looking eagerly at the shiny emblem.

"David!" Thatcher interrupted. "Isn't it a coincidence that the two of us have the same first name? You don't look Chinese.

In fact, except for CC, none of you look Chinese."

I cringed when I heard him. I knew how sensitive the three boys were about *this* subject. "So we are half-castes. What's so bad about that?" David answered defensively, bracing himself for an insult.

"Who said anything about it being bad?" Thatcher asked with a smile. "The ancestors of practically everyone in America came from someplace else. Diversity is what makes our country great."

"Sorry!" David said. "It's just that I've been insulted so many times before. Over here, people of mixed blood are called *za zhong*. We're the lowest of the low."

"And we have no parents," Marat added. "Children with parents look down on us. They treat us like oddballs. My desk partner at school told me the other day that normal children have parents who love them, whereas orphans turn weird because nobody wants us."

"Shanghai is not half as bad as Berlin," Sam said. "I was scared of everybody at school over there. My classmates used to gang up and play practical jokes on me. Someone would cough or spit in my face, squirt water on my head or put insects down the back of my shirt."

"You're from Berlin?" Thatcher asked in astonishment.

"Yes! I'm supposed to be a German boy!" Sam replied with a trace of bitterness. "But my father was Jewish and my mother Chinese. A true mongrel, that's me! Now my father and mother are both gone. Double jeopardy . . ."

"How come you ended up in Shanghai all by yourself?" Davenport asked.

"Because I had nowhere else to go. Shanghai is the only city in the world that doesn't require a visa to enter. It's the last place on earth that would accept a Jewish boy like me. The final refuge."

"Surely you weren't expelled from Germany because your mother was Chinese?" Thatcher asked.

"No," Sam replied sadly. "Because my father was Jewish. You know how the Nazis hate Jews. They arrested my father and sent him to a concentration camp. I think he's dead."

The airmen exchanged looks.

"Are the Nazis killing Jewish children too?" Thatcher sounded horrified.

"Jews of any age. There is a boy called Hans Friedman at my school who is about eighteen. I met him on the boat coming to Shanghai. He and his whole family were arrested in Berlin and packed like cattle into a train going to Auschwitz. The only reason he survived was because he had a Boy Scout's knife that included a small hacksaw. There was a window in the train with a steel bar. He worked on that bar the whole time he was on the train until he sawed through and escaped. Except for him, everyone on that train was killed."

"As a Christian, I'd say it was the will of God that Hans Friedman survived while the rest of his family died," Thatcher commented.

"My father was a Jew and my mother a Buddhist," Sam

replied. "Both of them would have agreed with you. I think differently. To me, Hans survived because he made a decision at a crucial moment to do something about his fate. Put a string of such events one after another and you will have guided the course of your own future."

"How brave you all are!" Davenport remarked. "To be risking your lives for strangers like us. I'm sure you know that you'll be in dire trouble if the Japanese find out what you're doing. Aren't you afraid?"

"Not really," Sam said with a wry look. "My mother is dead. My father was arrested by the Nazis four years ago, and I haven't heard from him since. Why should I fear death? Sometimes I think about it and wonder what comes afterward. The end came to my mother as peacefully as sleep. Where did she go? Did she turn into something else? Is she living in a quieter, darker and more peaceful place? Will I see her again when my time comes? I want to find out what happens next."

"I'd feel the same way if I knew for sure I'd come back to life again after I die," I said. "The problem with death is that it's so final. But perhaps that's what makes life wonderful—knowing it only happens once."

"I still don't know why you kids are helping us," McClure said. "What's in it for you?"

"I can only speak for myself," I said. "My mother died when I was five. My stepmother hates me. My father just wants to be left alone so he can make more money. All my life, I've yearned for things to be different so I won't feel left out. Finally, I've been given this chance to be included, to fight for a cause that I believe in."

"But why put yourselves out like this?" Lawson persisted. "The Japanese might even kill you for helping us. We owe you so much. How can we repay you?"

"What payment are you talking about? It is an honor to help you," David cried passionately. "What you've done is incredible! Our history books will be full of your daring deeds. Your story will be passed from generation to generation. You have struck a blow to the heart of the enemy. You have taken away their *Qi*. You have shown the bully that he can be beaten. You are heroes in the eyes of every Chinese!"

"Do all of you feel the same way?" Lawson asked. "There seems to be something special between you. . . ."

"Maybe it's because all of us have experienced discrimination in one form or another," Marat answered thoughtfully. "For as long as I can remember, I've dreamed of fighting battles on behalf of the underdog and righting the wrongs of those unjustly accused. Now that I know *kung fu*, I can finally do something about the injustice I see all around me."

"Perhaps this quest for justice is the bond that binds us," Sam said. "I do believe that injustice anywhere is a threat to equality and justice everywhere. I'm here to fight injustice too, just like you, Marat!"

"Isn't that exactly what you Americans are doing by bombing Japan and helping China's resistance fighters?" I asked fervently. "You remind me of the stories Big Aunt used to tell about the *you xia*, wandering knights-errant of old. The heroes risked their lives to help others also."

"I just hope the hatred ends," Thatcher said. "You know, kids, today is my birthday. I turned twenty-one today."

"You're only nine years older than me?" Marat was shocked. "I thought you were much, much older!"

"Twenty-one years old," I said, remembering the zodiac that Big Aunt had taught me the day before she left. "That means you were born in 1921, the year of the chicken. People born in the year of the chicken tend to be pioneers. You are devoted to your work and thirst after knowledge."

"How do you know that?" Thatcher asked with a smile. "Not that I'm contradicting you regarding my noble character, of course."

"According to our Chinese zodiac," I replied, "there are twelve years in a cycle. Each year is named after a different animal. The year 1921 was the year of the chicken. We Chinese believe that the year of a person's birth determines his personality. Although I don't know you very well, I have a chart that says that people born in the year of the chicken love to work and study."

"I was born in 1917," Lawson said. "What's my animal sign?"

"You were born in the year of the snake," Sam said quickly, before I could come up with the answer. "Snake people are wise and intense. We also tend to be temperamental. I said 'we' because I myself was born in the year of the snake."

"That means I'm exactly twelve years older than you," Lawson said.

"What's your animal sign, Marat?" Thatcher asked.

"The horse—"

"Born in 1930," I interrupted. "Just like me."

"I was born twelve years earlier, in 1918," Davenport said. "Does that mean I am also a horse person? What are we like?"

"Horse people are adventurous and loyal," said Sam, smiling at me.

We worked out that Clever was a tiger and McClure a dragon.

"I'm a dragon too!" David exclaimed. "We dragon people are supposed to be idealistic and responsible."

"Let's sing 'Happy Birthday' to Thatcher!" Davenport said. "Singing will make Lawson forget the pain in his leg."

We had just begun our song when the inner door flew open and Grandma Wu rushed in.

"What are you *doing*?" she demanded in an angry whisper. "Have all of you gone mad? Do you want the Japanese to hear you singing American songs at the top of your lungs?"

We looked sheepishly at one another. At that moment, there was a loud knocking. We were terrified and convinced that the Japanese had come for us. Grandma Wu approached the door gingerly. Then we heard a familiar male voice saying the password, *Chu sui san hu*, twice. It was morning, and Li Cha had returned.

CHAPTER 15

The Japanese Paratrooper

I CHA HAD BROUGHT long bamboo poles, sturdy ropes and ten young fishermen dressed in short pants, open shirts and sandals. The room was crowded with people.

"Tell the airmen that my men will carry them to the boat," Li Cha told us. "I know they're badly injured, but we need to get them off the island quickly. Unfortunately, we have no stretchers, so these latticed leather straps will have to do."

Under Li Cha's direction, the men cleared a space in the room and began to work. They tied short ropes to the corners of a square piece of latticed leather and turned it into a crude sort of litter. After testing the knots and making sure they were secure, the men slipped a long bamboo pole through the ends of the ropes. In this way, they built four makeshift stretchers. One by one, the injured airmen were lifted onto these contraptions,

139

each swaying under a pole balanced on the shoulders of two Chinese fishermen.

Thatcher, who was the least injured, chose to walk with the rest of us behind the stretcher bearers. Li Cha and Grandma Wu led the way in front. It was still dark when we started, but the faint light of dawn was slowly emerging. The weather cleared partially and red streaks of sunlight broke through from the east as we threaded our way along rice paddies and climbed a steep rocky hill, heading for the mountains. Behind us, the bright blue sea sparkled in the early morning sunshine beyond a sandy beach. It was the first time I'd seen a seashore in daylight, and I was thrilled at its serene splendor. I craned my neck to look but couldn't spot the crashed American plane.

We circled along a winding road and finally came out on the west side of the hill, which was called Niu Zhou Shan (Cow Continent Mountain). Below us was a beautiful green meadow, dotted with tall trees and brambly bushes. Between us and the meadow was a dense bamboo forest. As soon as Grandma Wu and Li Cha led the way into the forest, one of the stretcher bearers asked to stop. He needed to pee.

Thatcher and we children waited in the warm, patchy sunshine while the injured Americans and their stretcher bearers hid in the forest.

"Does your plane have a name?" David asked Thatcher.

"Yes. We call it the *Ruptured Duck*. Our friend Corporal Lovelace painted a Donald Duck, wearing a headset and earphones, in blue, yellow, white and red, on the fuselage. Below the duck he drew a pair of crutches. But our plane's lost in the ocean now. When Lawson was trying to land, the wheels must have hit a wave. The plane stopped so suddenly that the four guys in front shot out like cannonballs. I was in the back and found myself bouncing around like a Ping-Pong ball. The plane landed upside down, and I crawled out at the last minute through an emergency exit. Water rushed in, and I could hardly breathe. All I could think was that I didn't want to drown on my twenty-first birthday."

"I'm scared of the water too," I confided. "I can't swim."

"I'll teach you," David said. "The first thing to learn is to breathe through your mouth and not through your nose. That's how dolphins breathe, through the blow holes on top of their heads. Just watch them next time."

"Dolphins!" I protested. "How can you compare me to a fish? Besides, fish don't breathe through lungs. In my science class, I learned that fish have gills and get their oxygen directly from the water."

"A dolphin isn't a fish," David said. "Dolphins are mammals, just like you and me. They breathe the same way we do, through their lungs."

"How come you know so much about dolphins?" Thatcher asked.

"Because I'm used to swimming and playing with them," David replied. "When my parents were still alive, my mother used to bring me here to Nan Tian in the summer. There are lots of wild dolphins in these waters and I—"

Suddenly we heard the drone of an airplane overhead. Quick as a flash, Thatcher hit the ground and motioned us to do the same.

"Japanese naval patrol plane!" he whispered. "I can spot them anywhere. Hope they haven't seen us!"

The plane flew past our island, but then made a wide loop and circled back. We crawled behind bushes but kept our eyes fixed on the aircraft as it flew low over the coast. After a while, I saw the hatch of the plane open and a man jump out. He was so close, I could see his parachute ballooning open as he drifted down toward us.

Thatcher and Sam crawled into the forest to warn Li Cha and Grandma Wu, while Marat, David and I kept our eyes on the Japanese paratrooper. A strong gust of wind blew the parachute sideways toward the ocean. I made a fervent wish that the wind would dump him right into the middle of the East China Sea.

"I need to help Li Cha get the Americans away at once!" Grandma Wu said. She had her binoculars fixed on the paratrooper. "Go into the forest, children. If you see the Japanese airman, you must divert his attention so the Americans can escape. Cover our tracks!"

"What if we get lost, Grandma Wu?" Sam sounded panicky.

"Remember the compass button you sewed onto your warrior jacket? Let it guide you. Keep going in a southwesterly direction, and you will emerge from the forest on the side facing the mainland."

At first I felt scared, but I knew I mustn't let fear get the better of me. The boys were with me, and they were unbeatable at *kung fu*. I remembered David's dazzling moves during his fight with Johnny Fang. Besides, this could be my chance to use the skills I'd been practicing day after day. I was good at light walking and disguising my footprints now. But I didn't know whether I'd be able to keep up with the boys if we needed to climb a tree quickly or jump from branch to branch to get away.

The forest was misty and damp. I felt as if we were enveloped in a big cloud. The ground was thick with layers of fallen bamboo leaves, dense undergrowth, broken twigs and moss-covered stones. David, Marat, Sam and I used all our *kung fu* training to walk lightly and disguise the footprints left by the rest of our party. We raked the trodden leaves with our fingers, added fresh fronds, made false trails and created misleading paths.

It started to drizzle, and the woods turned dark and forbidding. Nobody felt like talking. The only sound was that of our footsteps plopping against the squishy mud. I was seized by nameless fears: all the bad things I'd ever worried about rolled into one, and then some. Shadows moving on the walls of my bedroom at night. Footsteps coming up the stairs when I was alone in the dark. Rats darting out of hidden corners. Creatures lurking under my bed. Insects crawling beneath the sheets waiting to bite me.

"Halt!" someone shouted. We jumped and spun around. At first we saw no one. Then a young man emerged from behind a clump of bamboo. He was neatly dressed in the uniform of a Japanese air force officer, and he held a revolver.

He was as startled as we were. Four children playing in the forest. Or were we?

"An American plane crash-landed on your island yesterday," he said in broken Chinese with a heavy Japanese accent. "My captain and I saw the wreckage from the sky. Have you seen or heard anything?"

None of us dared to answer. Our prolonged silence became awkward and embarrassing. After a while, I began to sweat even though I was trembling from cold and fear. Then, unexpectedly, Marat stepped forward and said in a clear voice, "We don't know what you're talking about. We can't understand you."

The Japanese paratrooper was obviously taken aback by Marat's confident manner. He glanced at the revolver in his hand and started to point the gun at us, but then thought better of it and put it back in his holster.

I breathed again. But what was he thinking? That he would have no trouble overpowering a bunch of frightened children? That kids didn't deserve to be shot? That it would look foolish to be brandishing a gun when no one was challenging him?

Then I noticed how young he was. His cheeks were smooth, and he looked as if he hadn't begun to shave yet. He couldn't have been more than eighteen years old!

I felt my mouth go dry and my heart race as he stood hesitantly in front of us. Would he arrest us and take us to Bridge House, like Marat's brother, Ivanov? If it came to a fight, would we be able to beat him with our *kung fu* skills? Would he kill us?

Suddenly, in the tense silence, a most unexpected sound erupted. Everyone heard it. We looked at one another in astonishment. Who had produced it?

It seemed to have come from one of the boys. Could Marat really have farted? Marat the fastidious, who insisted on bathing daily in cold water even while on the road? There now came a stench so potent that all of us moved slightly away while Marat looked at the ground, extremely embarrassed.

At that moment, David began to laugh uncontrollably. His mirth was that of a mischievous child: spontaneous, devoid of malice and contagious. Great peals of laughter rippled out and one by one, we all joined in, including the Japanese officer and Marat himself. We couldn't help ourselves.

In some mysterious way, our crazy outburst seemed to clear the air and unite us. Outwardly nothing had changed, and yet everything was different. We didn't see how someone who had just laughed with us would now try to harm us.

"I'm so sorry," Marat mumbled in Japanese, stepping forward and holding out his hand. "My stomach has been bothering me. I'm Marat Yoshida, and these are my friends, CC, David and Sam."

"You speak Japanese!" the Japanese officer sounded relieved and delighted as he shook Marat's hand. "I don't speak much Chinese. I'm Kenshio Yamada. Are you Japanese?"

"Yes," said Marat. "Me and my friends are here on vacation. How can we help you?"

Just then we heard a loud rustling and the splintering of twigs. Who could be lurking nearby?

"Hello! Who's there?" Sam called out loudly in a shaky voice.

Kenshio Yamada put his finger to his lips. "Tell your friend to keep quiet!" he whispered to Marat in Japanese. He took out his revolver. Then he said in broken Chinese, "Listen! Someone heavy is moving behind the bamboo. Maybe it's an American!"

It was true! We could hear heavy footsteps trudging through the forest. Surely Thatcher wouldn't have come back! Or would he? Did he forget something? Was he crazy?

"Oh, no! Oh, no!" Sam moaned. I couldn't tell whether Sam was groaning for the American or for our newfound Japanese friend.

"Quiet!" Kenshio whispered furiously. "Don't be such a baby! He'll hear you!"

"Maybe it's not a man but an animal . . ." Sam began tremulously. Then he let out a shriek that made the hairs rise on the back of my head. "Ah!!!!! Yaaaaa!!!!!"

"What?" I asked, frantically looking around. "What did you see?"

"Over there! Something enormous!" Sam pointed to a thick cluster of bamboo. "I saw it move! It's not a man. It's a monster!"

CHAPTER 16

The Monster

 MONSTER?" Kenshio sounded bewildered.

"Look!" David pointed to the ground.

There, between the fallen bamboo leaves on the far left, was a clear imprint in the mud. Marat ran forward, knelt by the mud and examined it carefully. We heard him counting softly: "One, two, three, four, five, six!"

"Six toes!" Marat reported shakily. "Nobody has a foot with six toes! It's not the footprint of a human being! This was made by the paw of something spooky. An alien or a weird brute of some sort! I thought I saw it just now too. Sam's right! It *is* a monster."

"Monster!" Sam whispered, trembling like a leaf. "Mother told me a story once about Samnaja, the Abominable Monster of Tibet. It's a fantastic beast that's really a demon. It has pointed ears that go straight up, like horns. And four short tusks protruding from a mouth that can spew out smoke and fire when it gets angry. Its wrinkled brown body is covered with black hairs and colored spots. And each enormous forepaw has five fingers plus a thumb, just like this pawprint. It sits high up on the branch of a tree and lies in wait for small animals and children. Then it swoops down like a dragon and pounces—"

"Stop it!" Kenshio commanded. "You're scaring yourself to death with your imagination!"

"This pawprint didn't come from Sam's imagination," David pointed out logically. "It has six toes, just like Sam's Abominable Monster of Tibet!"

"What shall we do?" I asked.

"Let's see if we can find more pawprints and follow them," Kenshio said. "I don't believe in monsters. This could be a trick to scare us away. If we come across your Abominable Monster, Sam, I promise to pump it full of bullets before it can do you harm."

We found a trail of six-toed pawprints leading deep into the forest. Some prints were deeply etched into the mud, but others were faint. The rest were lost among tree roots, pine needles, bamboo leaves, ferns, moss and fallen branches. As we trudged along, I felt confused. Weren't the Japanese supposed to be our enemy? If so, why were we following a Japanese paratrooper? Maybe this was a plan to distract Kenshio from finding the Americans. But Sam had seemed genuinely scared when he saw the creature lurking behind the bamboo. Was it all an act?

For half an hour, we followed the pawprints into the heart of the forest, until the foliage overhead was so thick that I could hardly see the sky. Bamboos twice as high as a man were interspersed with hemlock, beech, fir and thickets of rhododendron. The rhododendron blossoms were a dazzle of crimson, yellow, white, purple and silvery pink.

Kenshio suddenly stopped and crouched down. We all searched but could find no more pawprints. Sam's Tibetan monster had vanished in midstride.

Although Kenshio and the boys were with me, I felt a wave of fear. The air carried a rank, wild odor, reminding me of elephants at the zoo. Could I actually smell the monster, or was this just my imagination? I sensed that the creature was not only close by but was watching me. Then a fierce wind sprang up, making the trees creak and groan. The first drops of rain wet my face. A flash of lightning threw the branches into stark relief. In the sudden glare I glimpsed a hulking shape sitting on top of a tree immediately in front of me.

"David!" I screamed. "There's something up there. It's huge and black—"

Thunder cracked, and the forest seemed to open up as rain came pouring down. The eye of the storm was directly above us.

"Don't be scared," Kenshio said as lightning flashed again. "I saw the thing in the treetop just now. I'm glad I didn't shoot it with my pistol! That's no monster!"

"What is it?" I asked fearfully.

"I should have known!" Kenshio answered, patting me on the head. "After all, I was studying zoology at Tokyo University when I got drafted. The creature sitting up there is the national treasure of China. It's a *giant panda*!"

CHAPTER 17

Master Wu's Pet

**HAT A RELIEF!** As soon as Kenshio told us that Sam's Abominable Monster was really a panda, I felt so much better. I screwed up my eyes and looked again. Sure enough! Perched on a forked branch of the tree immediately facing us was the distinct white-and-black face of a giant panda. With her chin resting on her hands and her head cocked to one side, she was observing us quietly from among the leaves. Despite her size, she looked so cuddly and cute that I wanted to talk to her.

"Hello, panda! How did *you* get up there so high?"

"She's not going to answer you," Kenshio said. "Pandas are very shy. But I've got something in my pocket left over from lunch that might tempt her to come down. Pandas love sweet potatoes."

He waved the potato back and forth, but the panda ignored him. Instead, she grabbed a nearby stalk of bamboo with her front paw, bit off a piece with her teeth and began stripping off the tough outer covering to get to the pith. We all craned our necks for a closer look as she delicately ate the bamboo. Meanwhile, the rain eased as the storm passed over us.

"She doesn't seem quite real," I said. "She's like something out of a dream."

"She has the face of a teddy bear but sits upright like a person," Marat said. "I love her big black eyes and black ears on top of her white baby face and black body."

"Big, gentle and round, sitting there not making a sound!" David said. Kenshio handed the sweet potato to David, who began waving it at the panda again.

"She lives by herself in the forest like a hermit," Kenshio said. "She doesn't harm anyone, but hunters kill her for her skin. There aren't many pandas left. We need to protect her so she doesn't get hurt."

The panda began to climb down. She embraced the trunk and lowered herself tail first, carrying out a series of looping movements with her soles against the bark. When she reached the ground, she backed up to the same tree and raised her tail. Balancing her weight on her two front paws, she did a handstand. Then she rubbed her bottom up and down against the tree trunk.

"She is marking that tree with her scent to tell other pandas that she was here first. That's how she claims her territory," said Kenshio.

The panda now sat down on her haunches against the tree, stretched out her right front paw and accepted the sweet potato from David's hand. David grinned with satisfaction and raised both his fists in triumph. Keeping her eyes on David the whole time, the panda began to eat. Her white belly was fully exposed, and her black legs were splayed out in front. Her black ears twitched back and forth as she chewed, obviously relishing every bite.

A piece of potato dropped onto her belly as she ate. She used her thumb and five fingers to pick it up and pop it back into her mouth.

Our interval of peace was suddenly broken by the wail of a siren, followed by the drone of an airplane. Startled, Kenshio looked at his watch and hit his forehead with his palm.

"Have I been here for two hours already? It feels as if I've just arrived." He took out a map and compass from his pocket. "The gunboat *Isamuru* is picking me up. If I don't appear soon, they'll send a patrol to look for me. Good-bye, all of you. What a surprising day this has been! Not only did I see a live panda in the wild; I also made some unexpected friends."

"We've never met a Japanese paratrooper before," said David. "Are they all like you?"

"Japan is a big place with millions of people," Kenshio answered. "Everyone is different. There are many honorable people in my country. Personally, I hate this war, but I was drafted, so I had no choice. I'm really glad I didn't have to kill or arrest any Americans today. I have to go now, but I hope we'll meet again after this war is over." He clicked his heels and bowed to us before hurrying away.

* * *

The encounter with the panda and Kenshio had exhausted us. We sat on the ground in silence for a long time, too tired to talk. I stared at my compass button and was planning to walk in a southwesterly direction when we heard someone playing a flute in the distance. Music filled the forest and seemed to pull all the rustling bamboos, rhododendron flowers and fir tree branches toward it.

"Perhaps it's Master Wu!" David said. "Not many people can play the flute like that."

"Look at the panda," I said.

The panda had gathered a bunch of bamboo around her, but now she stopped munching and began walking slowly toward the music on all fours, then rolling and tumbling and making happy noises. I was so involved with the panda's antics that it took me a while to notice a flute-playing man, followed by someone else, emerging through the mist. I took a proper look and saw that it was *indeed* Master Wu and—

"Big Aunt!" I shouted as I ran toward her. She met me halfway and caught me in her arms. Both of us were crying with happiness. I felt giddy with joy as she hugged me. A lifetime seemed to have gone by since I had last seen her.

"My precious little treasure!" she said over and over.

Master Wu smiled at the panda, which was licking his hand like a gentle puppy. Then I remembered the photo of the pet panda he had brought over from Sichuan Province as a baby. "Master Wu," I said. "Is this Mei Mei?"

Master Wu laughed. "Of course! Isn't she pretty? Just look at her."

As if on cue, Mei Mei stood up and leaned her left forearm against a tree. With her right hand, she pushed a stalk of bamboo into her mouth like a pipe and peeled off the outer sheath by twisting it against her teeth. Biting off pieces of the tender pith, she chewed each morsel separately until the entire stalk was eaten. Then she clasped her hands in front of her face, licked them clean and wiped her mouth like a cat.

David and Marat told Master Wu about meeting Kenshio and how they had recognized Mei Mei's footprints but pretended she was a monster. I clung to my aunt and told her everything that had happened since our parting. It was wonderful to be with her again.

"Your smile is so wide, it's running around your face eight times!" Master Wu said to me at last. "I'm sorry I have to interrupt your reunion. The American airmen need you, and so does my mother, Grandma Wu. We have to join them before sailing to the mainland."

"Will you come with us, Big Aunt?" I begged. I couldn't bear to be parted from her now that I'd found her again.

"No. I'm sorry, I can't. Not yet."

"Then can I stay here with you?"

"That isn't possible either, I'm afraid. Otherwise your father and stepmother might accuse me of kidnapping you. Strange as it may seem, you'd probably make your stepmother happier by wandering around Shanghai as a homeless refugee than living here with me in Nan Tian."

"Why does Niang hate me so much?"

"She wants to control you. You are too independent for her."

"When will you come back to Shanghai, Big Aunt?" I asked.

"I'm not sure," she answered. "There's so much to do here. Grandma Liu still needs me and . . . I've become heavily involved with the resistance movement in Nan Tian. Besides, you're getting an excellent education at the Martial Arts Academy with Grandma Wu."

"We really must go, children!" Master Wu insisted. "Let me show you my shortcut."

Master Wu led us to an opening between a twisted old pine tree and a craggy rock. He pushed away fallen branches and debris to reveal a hidden stairway covered by a grated lid. One by one the boys climbed down into a steep, narrow tunnel.

Big Aunt held me tightly.

"Can't you come with us?" I begged her one last time.

Her eyes were sad. "No, my precious. I must go. We have four seriously wounded Americans on our hands. They can't walk and they need medical attention. I must send a message to Dr. Chen by pigeon post as soon as possible. Besides, it's best if you don't know where I am in case you're questioned."

I fished Lawson's pilot badge out of my pocket and gave it to her. "This is my most precious possession in the whole world," I said. "The American pilot, Ted Lawson, gave it to me last night. It's a symbol of friendship between China and America. I want you to keep it for me until I've grown up."

As I entered the tunnel with Master Wu, I looked back one last time and saw Big Aunt and Mei Mei outlined against the forest. Big Aunt was holding Mei Mei's left paw with one hand and waving good-bye to me with the other.

The tunnel was steep, dark and damp but thankfully very short. When we came out, we were already halfway down a hill on the southwest side of the island. Immediately below us was an imposing Buddhist temple, painted red. Its dark gray slate roof had pointy corners that tilted upward on either side. Its carved wooden front door and windows were elegantly decorated with trelliswork. Two stone lions guarded the temple gate, one on each side. In front of them stood several well-armed guerrilla soldiers dressed in civilian clothes. They were protecting the wounded American airmen. Thatcher was talking to Grandma Wu and Li Cha, who appeared to be the man in charge. From time to time, small groups of men would run up and report to him. As soon as we arrived, Master Wu joined them, and they conferred urgently for a few minutes. Then Grandma Wu and Master Wu took us aside.

"We've received information that a scouting force of eighty-five Japanese soldiers has arrived on the island," Grandma Wu said. "They're searching for the Americans. Master Wu needs to leave immediately to deal with the situation. Please say good-bye now. We'll have a quick lunch here and be on our way."

Li Cha ordered food, and Grandma Wu gave us bowls of sautéed bean curd over rice and cups of piping hot water. After lunch, we set off toward the harbor. Six rifle-carrying guerrillas marched alongside the four wounded airmen borne on stretchers. Word of the Americans' bombing raid had already spread. Everywhere wide-eyed villagers gazed at our procession with respect. Many of the children stood at attention and some even saluted. The airmen responded by giving the children chewing gum, pens, coins and buttons torn off their coats.

By late afternoon, we reached the southernmost tip of the island. I could hear the cry of the seagulls and smell the clean, bracing air of the ocean. In front of me an expanse of blue water stretched out to infinity. In the afternoon sunset, a junk sailed slowly toward us from the mainland. As it came close to shore, Grandma Wu called out our password to the sailors, and they responded by saying *Wang Qin bi Chu*, four times. We ran toward the boat, buoyed by a frenzy of excitement at accomplishing our mission. We were going to sail away from the island with the Americans!

But our joy was short-lived. From the direction of the junk came a clear high whistle. Someone shouted, "Dire emergency!" Without a word, our guerrilla guards grabbed the bamboo poles from the porters and lowered the wounded Americans into a muddy ditch that ran parallel to the sea. Quick as a flash, Grandma Wu jumped in after them and ordered everyone to do the same. She flattened herself on the ground and held a finger to her lips.

I crawled beside her and carefully raised my head to look. A gleaming white gunboat shot out from behind a sandy promontory, the red insignia of the rising sun of Japan clearly visible on the ship's hull. My heart pounded against my chest. The two boats were now side by side. A million thoughts went through my head. Had the Japanese found the remains of the crashed plane? Did someone betray us? Surely it wasn't Kenshio? What if the Japanese had seen us jump into the ditch?

Now I could hear voices. The Japanese were questioning the men in the junk. They sounded arrogant, the conquerors addressing the vanquished. I was sure we were doomed. These fishermen were so very poor. I remembered their bare feet and torn clothing. Some were certainly close to starvation. Could anyone blame them for turning us in for money?

I hid my face in my arms and plugged my ears. It was awful, lying helplessly in the ditch, waiting. My hands were clammy, and sweat ran down my neck. After what seemed to be an eternity, someone poked me in the elbow. Slowly, I opened my eyes.

"It's a miracle!" David was whispering. "They're going away!"

We waited until the sound of the gunboat faded. Then we climbed out and sprinted toward the junk. The guerrillas helped carry the Americans onto the boat, jumping in only after everyone had boarded. They cocked their guns warily as the boat pulled up its anchor and moved away. Lawson tried to pay them, but they shook their heads and wouldn't accept any money. One of them whispered, "It's not necessary. We know what you've done for China."

At that moment, I felt very proud to be Chinese.

CHAPTER 18

Escape to the Mainland

T FIRST, WE HAD a breeze. The sails were hoisted, and the junk gathered speed. We children remained on deck because the main cabin was so crowded. Grandma Wu rolled down the bamboo blinds at the sides to hide the wounded Americans lying on the floor. After a while, the boat slowed down. Grandma Wu scanned the sea anxiously through her binoculars.

"Our boat is almost at a standstill," she said in a worried voice. "This is terrible!"

David and Marat looked at each other. Without a word, David pulled out the flute dangling on a chain around his neck and began to play a stirring tune. I didn't know the words of his song, but the music sounded familiar. Where had I heard it before? The lilting melody was a testimony against oppression, a prayer for justice and a plea for freedom. Each note went straight to my heart and lingered there.

While David played, Marat scanned the ocean waves. Not long afterward, a black shape emerged from the water and surged rapidly toward us. Marat began jumping up and down with glee.

"Ling Ling! Ling Ling!" he chanted loudly. Sam and I soon joined him.

David kept playing, but I could see his eyes sparkling with happiness. We watched the dolphin's sleek, streamlined body as it swam at breakneck speed, drawn by David's music like a nail to a magnet.

"Ling Ling to the rescue!" Marat shouted as the dolphin leapt in the air and splashed back into the water right next to the junk. David gently scratched Ling Ling with an oar. She reared and rolled over in the water, as if suggesting that David should now pet her belly. Everyone laughed.

Meanwhile, the wind had died down completely, and the light was fading fast. The boat rocked gently in the water. We were becalmed. The sailors started to row, but progress was agonizingly slow.

There was a bucket of small fish on deck, and David tossed a few to Ling Ling who jumped to catch them. She sprang playfully into the air several more times before submerging herself and turning over once more. This time, David gave her underside a long rub with his oar.

"Stop playing, David!" Grandma Wu commanded, her eyes fixed on her binoculars. "There's something on the horizon.

Let's hope it's not the Japanese patrol boat we saw earlier."

"I'm not playing!" David protested emphatically. "I called Ling Ling here to help us! Last summer, Grandma Liu, Marat, Ling Ling and I practiced this routine for hours and hours. I'm going to show you. Wish me luck!"

He stripped down to his shorts and put on a life jacket. Under Marat's direction, we attached a large rubber ring-shaped life preserver to a rope, which we tied firmly to the deck, then we threw the ring overboard. Ling Ling hovered around the boat, making an insistent clicking sound as she swam.

"She's scanning the water," David explained to me. "When the clicks hit the rubber ring, they'll echo back to her. That's how she finds things in water. She's listening for those echo-clicks."

With Marat's help, David climbed onto the railing and positioned himself above the water, getting ready to dive. Ling Ling splashed around beneath him. *Click! Click! Click! Click!* David counted to three, then jumped overboard and climbed onto Ling Ling's back. At the same moment, I saw Ling Ling slide her snout through the rubber ring.

"That gunboat is definitely Japanese!" Grandma Wu was shouting. "I can see the sign of the rising sun. It's heading right for us. Full speed ahead!"

David whistled sharply as he grabbed Ling Ling's dorsal fin with one hand and clutched the rope between the junk and the dolphin's snout with the other. Ling Ling moved her tail up and down energetically in response. I could hardly believe what I was seeing! David was riding on Ling Ling's back as if she was a horse! Boy and dolphin zoomed through the water together, pulling the junk behind them like a dog on a leash. It was an amazing sight!

The Japanese gunboat kept following us. No matter how hard Ling Ling and David pulled, they couldn't shake it loose. Ling Ling started to make a sharp, high, eerie, whistling sound.

"Why is Ling Ling making that noise?" I called out fearfully to Marat. "It gives me the creeps!"

"That's her way of calling for help," Marat replied. "I heard it only once before. The day we found her. She was bleeding and had a fishhook stuck in her back. . . . Hey! What's that swimming toward us? I think it's Bumby! Grandma Wu, let me have your binoculars for a second! Yes! Yes! It's definitely Bumby!"

"Who's Bumby?" Sam and I asked in unison as we saw a huge black pilot whale rapidly approaching our boat, seemingly from nowhere.

"Bumby is Ling Ling's cousin!" Marat shouted happily. "They swim together all the time. He weighs more than two thousand pounds. He'll show the Japanese a thing or two!"

Bumby submerged himself under the water behind our junk and waited patiently until the Japanese gunboat was almost on top of him. Then he surfaced and went to work.

When he butted the ship's hull with his enormous head, the boat listed dangerously to one side. Before we realized what was happening, Bumby dived down and disappeared from view. He must have been batting his tail beneath the water because giant waves began rocking the gunboat violently from side to side. The vessel was about to capsize when it suddenly reversed its course and sped away in the direction of Nan Tian Island.

We cheered loudly and clapped our hands at the sight of the Japanese gunboat retreating. Thatcher came on deck. He gave us the thumbs-up sign and taught us a new American expression to celebrate our escape. We shouted "Hip! Hip! Hooray!" at the tops of our voices whenever he raised his arm. Soon everyone on board was bellowing "Hip! Hip! Hooray!" when Thatcher gave the signal, even Grandma Wu, the American airmen and the fishermen. It was exhilarating.

Meanwhile, Ling Ling and David continued pulling us. They guided us across *San Men Wan* (Three Doors Bay), up the *Hai Men* (Sea Gate) Estuary to *Yong Quan* (Gushing Spring) Port on the mainland. Night had already fallen when our junk finally scraped against a concrete wharf. David stroked Ling Ling and detached the rubber ring from her snout. Standing on her back, he clung to the rope with both hands and hauled himself onto the deck.

"Ling Ling is waiting for her reward," Grandma Wu said. "Why don't you feed her the rest of the fish in the bucket?"

Ling Ling bobbed up beside the junk with her mouth wide open in anticipation. There were still eight fish left, so the four of us had the pleasure of giving Ling Ling two fish each. She swallowed them whole, without chewing. Then, with a satisfied flick of her tail, she headed back to sea.

We had been saved from the Japanese by a dolphin! It felt

like something out of a fairy tale. I thought of the ancient Tang dynasty story of Chinese Cinderella that Master Wu had told me. Not only did the heroine and I share the same name, Ye Xian, but she too had been protected from harm by a fish. What a coincidence! Even though a dolphin wasn't exactly a fish, I couldn't help feeling that I had well and truly earned my nickname, CC.

As soon as we stepped onto the pier, we saw four surgical stretchers made of wood and canvas laid out neatly in a row.

"That's impressive, isn't it, David?" I commented. "News of the four wounded American airmen has already spread to *Yong Quan* Port via the grapevine."

"Over here the grapevine is called the bamboo wireless!" Sam quipped.

"It's more likely that the stretchers were brought here by our local agents, after my son and CC's Big Aunt sent them an urgent request by pigeon express," Grandma Wu informed us proudly. "The two of them know every hiding place and shortcut on Nan Tian. They've set up a system of secret signals that can be passed quickly from island to mainland and back again."

Eight stretcher bearers appeared, carrying paper lanterns on long poles. They stuck the poles into their belts, hoisted the airmen onto the stretchers and transported them through the narrow, unlit streets to the local China Relief Station. Thatcher and the rest of us followed on foot. David was so exhausted that Sam and Marat practically had to carry him. We were told that although Yong Quan was supposed to be under Japanese control, the local puppet troops governing the port were sympathetic toward the Americans.

A group of nurses bandaged the Americans' wounds and washed the blood off their faces. We were offered hot tea and sweet rice cakes, but I was too tired to eat. I was so relieved when the nurses brought in cushions and blankets. We spent the night sleeping on the floor.

We were woken by the sound of a loud voice. It was Dr. Chen, the physician from Chuchow, talking animatedly to the Americans in fluent English. He examined their wounds, shaking his head in dismay.

"We need to get you to my father's hospital in Linhai as soon as possible," Dr. Chen said to Lawson. "Your leg is badly infected. I'm afraid of gangrene."

"How far is Linhai?"

"Twenty-six miles. Normally, it would take less than an hour by bus from Yong Quan. Since the Japanese are inspecting every vehicle on the major roads out of town, I've brought twelve men and six sedan chairs. We're going to Linhai by a different route in the old-fashioned way: by taking the number 11 express train!"

"What do you mean?"

"That's another way of saying we'll use our legs and hike around the hills."

"Is that how you got here?" Thatcher asked.

"Same number 11 train. We walked all night. The journey took twelve hours."

"But you've just arrived! Surely you need to rest?" Lawson was shocked.

"We must leave at once," Dr. Chen replied, "otherwise you'll risk getting captured."

"But you haven't slept. . . ."

Dr. Chen shook his head and stared with respect at Lawson's bashed-in face and purple leg. "We know what you men have sacrificed for China. It's my honor to return the favor, at least in part."

Once again, Lawson emptied his pockets and tried to give all his money to the staff who had taken care of him. But they handed it back and said they wanted nothing. Instead, they helped the injured Americans and Grandma Wu into five of the sedan chairs. Thatcher chose to walk and said he would take turns with everyone else to ride in the last remaining chair.

Dr. Chen led the way, accompanied by Thatcher and the four of us. The sedan chair carriers followed in a single file down the confined, dusty alleyways. At first nobody chose to ride in the sixth chair, but we soon changed our minds. The journey seemed interminable.

As we walked across rice fields, up and down hillocks and through village after village, I was glad to find a few hard biscuits in my pockets and a canteen of water. Ahead of us, Thatcher questioned Dr. Chen about the fate of the other American airmen who had raided Tokyo.

"There were sixteen planes in the raid, each with a crew of five men," Thatcher was saying. "Lawson thinks that every plane must have run out of fuel. Do you know what happened to the others? Especially our leader, Jimmy Doolittle?"

"Not a single American plane was shot down," Dr. Chen answered. "Besides your plane, the *Ruptured Duck*, one plane flew to Russia and landed safely in Vladivostok. Of the remaining fourteen, the crews from eleven of the planes bailed out and descended by parachute. Those who survived are on their way to Chungking. This included your leader, Jimmy Doolittle. The twelfth plane crashed on an island close to Nan Tian, but luckily all five airmen survived. Li Cha and Master Wu are trying to get them to the mainland. One of them is a doctor who'll be able to help your pilot Lawson, with the injured leg. Unfortunately, we believe that the last two planes crashed in Japanese-occupied territory and their crews were taken prisoner."

"Where would they take them?" Thatcher asked.

"Our agents tell us that all captured American airmen are being sent to Bridge House in Shanghai for special interrogation."

"Bridge House!" cried Thatcher in dismay. "These Americans are prisoners of war. They shouldn't be incarcerated in a torture chamber. We were briefed about Bridge House before the raid. Isn't it a hell on earth?"

"Your raid over Tokyo has humiliated the Japanese, and they want revenge," Dr. Chen said. "I'm afraid they might do terrible things to the prisoners."

Thatcher said nothing.

Then David asked, "Can we help?"

"I was talking to Grandma Wu about that. She should take you children back to Shanghai as soon as possible," Dr. Chen answered. "You've done a great job getting the crew of the *Ruptured Duck* out of Nan Tian. What our American friends need now is medical care, which I can provide only at my father's hospital in Linhai. Mr. Lawson's leg is infected and may have to be amputated before he can be moved to Chungking. But I'm worried that the Japanese will be out hunting for them and their rescuers. That includes the four of you."

"Oh, no!" David demurred. "We want to accompany Mr. Lawson to the hospital. Besides, Mr. Thatcher hasn't finished telling us how everything works in his plane yet. He drew a sketch of the instrument panel and—"

"Your mission was to rescue the Americans and lead them to safety," Dr. Chen interrupted firmly. "You've accomplished this. If you go back to school now and don't tell anyone where you've been, the Japanese will have no reason to suspect you. On the other hand, if you stay with the airmen at my father's hospital, you'll be more of a burden than a help. Grandma Wu has already booked train tickets for herself and all of you from Linhai back to Shanghai. If she has her way, you'll be sitting at your school desks the day after tomorrow."

CHAPTER 19

A Visitor from Home

**AKING UP IN SHANGHAI** after an exhausting journey that took three days, I couldn't remember where I was, only that it felt wonderful to be lying on a bed with a pillow under my head. Someone was moving around the room, but I kept my eyes shut, reluctant to wake up completely.

Was it all a dream? I asked myself. Did I go to Nan Tian Island and rescue five American airmen? Did I see a giant panda leaning against a tree and feeding herself bamboo with her own paws? Did a dolphin pull our boat safely to the mainland? When I open my eyes again, where will I be? Is that Niang I hear snooping around in my room, finding fault and gathering evidence against me?

"CC! CC! Wake up! There's a woman at the door asking for you."

I opened my eyes and saw Grandma Wu's worried face looking down at me.

I sprang out of bed, ran to the door and yanked it open. Ah Yee was standing there by herself, wringing her hands and looking anxious.

"Miss Ye Xian!" she cried. "I'm sorry to disturb you so early in the morning. Your father is finally asking for you to come home—"

"Finally!" I shouted angrily as I let her into Grandma Wu's Academy. "What do you mean, *finally*? Don't you understand that I don't *want* to go home? I'm perfectly happy here."

"Maybe it's *me* who wants you to come home. What does it matter? Did you forget it was your father's birthday yesterday? He celebrated by giving a big party. All his friends and relatives came. Many of them asked for you and were surprised you weren't there. After the party was over, your father sat in the living room for a long time, drinking by himself. Your stepmother had gone to bed. I knew he was thinking of you, so I brought him a cup of tea and stood there talking to him about the old days when your mama was still alive. One topic led to another. After a while, he agreed that I should go to your aunt's apartment first thing this morning and tell you to come home."

"So it was *your* idea that I should go home and not *his*," I said resentfully.

"What does it matter whose idea it was to begin with? At least he wants you home *now*!"

"What does Niang say?"

"I have no idea. I'm not concerned about her. It's you and your father I worry about. And he has ordered me to bring you home. He loves you and misses you!"

"Did he actually say that?" I asked, overwhelmed by a sudden rush of emotion.

"Not in so many words, but I could read the expression on his face. Sometimes it's hard for men to admit certain things . . . especially when it involves their wives and daughters. Surely you're aware of that?"

"I suppose . . ."

"Well, are you coming home with me now?"

"I—I don't know what to do. . . . What if I refuse?"

"Oh, Miss Ye Xian. Don't make trouble for yourself and for everyone else! Do you remember what your niang said when they first threw you out?"

"What did she say?"

"She said that if your aunt doesn't let you go when your father sends for you, they'll sue her for kidnapping you. If you don't come home with me today, they're bound to blame everything on your aunt. You know as well as I do what your stepmother is capable of. She'd like nothing better than to cause trouble between you, your aunt, your father and your friends."

"I'm afraid you're right," I agreed reluctantly. "Please wait here. I need to talk to my teacher, Grandma Wu."

It didn't take Grandma Wu long to advise that I needed to go home with Ah Yee.

"Just be careful!" she said. "Keep your wits about you. Stop by the bookstall in the bazaar on your way home from school this afternoon. I'll be there waiting for you."

I dressed in my school uniform, took my schoolbag and went home by rickshaw with Ah Yee. Niang was still asleep when we arrived. Father looked both happy and relieved to see me. He wore a business suit and was dashing out to attend a meeting when Ah Yee and I almost collided with him at the front door.

He and I looked at each other, and I felt a terrible ache in my heart. I had forgotten how distinguished and handsome he was. All the time I lived at home and we were together, I'd never really "seen" him. He was simply there, seemingly present and accessible but actually increasingly remote. Today I noticed everything about him: the worry lines on his forehead, the white hairs at his temples, the slightly stooped shoulders, the soft paunch below his belt, the scratch mark on his chin where he had cut himself shaving. I longed to throw my arms around him and tell him I loved him. Instead, I stood there and said nothing.

The long silence was embarrassing. He finally coughed nervously and said, "How tall you've grown! Did you have a good time at your aunt's place?"

"It was all right," I mumbled morosely.

"Are you glad to be home?"

"Oh, yes. Thank you so much, Father," I said sarcastically, but he didn't seem to notice.

"Well, I'm glad you're home too," he said absentmindedly as he went out the door.

I climbed the stairs to my room by myself and sat on my bed. For some reason, I started to cry. I thought of everything I had experienced since I had last seen him: my wonderful *kung fu* lessons at the academy; my weekly column in the newsletter; my great teacher, Grandma Wu; my new friends, David, Sam and Marat; my secret double life; my journey to Nan Tian and the exciting rescue of the American airmen. . . . Yet, in spite of it all, the only thing I'd ever really wanted was that my father should think well of me.

I went to school as usual. Nobody seemed to notice anything different about me, except my best friend, Wu Chun-mei. She and I were in the habit of telling each other everything we did when we were apart, so she kept asking where I'd been and what I'd done while I was away. Not knowing what to say without lying, I finally told her I'd gone to help a sick relative who had broken her leg. I felt terrible saying this and my hands got sweaty, but she didn't seem to notice.

As soon as school was over, I dashed over to the bookstall. To my delight, I found Grandma Wu and David reading on the bench. They greeted me warmly.

"Grandma Wang has gone to do some errands, but she'll be back in an hour. David was given the afternoon off from school today. He wanted to accompany me. Sam and Marat asked me to say hello to you."

"I daren't stay too long," I said. "I haven't seen my stepmother yet. She was still asleep when I left for school this morning.

173

Please send a note by pigeon to Big Aunt in Nan Tian. Tell her I'm back at my parents' place, but she's not to worry. Will you ask her when she's coming back to Shanghai?"

"I received a letter by pigeon from your aunt just before lunch today," Grandma Wu said. "I'm afraid Grandma Liu has taken a turn for the worse. Big Aunt says she won't be back till the beginning of June at the earliest."

"Oh, no!" I groaned. "What about the crew of the *Ruptured Duck* and poor Mr. Lawson's injured leg? Did they get away from Linhai?"

"The sad news is that Mr. Lawson's leg had to be amputated," Grandma Wu said. "The good news is that he has already recovered from his operation. All five airmen from the *Ruptured Duck* are being flown to Chungking as we speak."

"Yes! Fantastic! We did it!" David and I grinned at each other. "Hip! Hip! Hooray!"

"What about the Americans who were captured by the Japanese? Any news?" I continued.

"Marat got another secret letter from Ivanov today—" Grandma Wu began.

"Did he write it in invisible ink again?" I interrupted breathlessly.

"Of course!" David replied with aplomb. "Only this time Grandma Wu let us take turns holding the hot iron above the paper!"

"Lucky you! Wish I had been there too!" I turned to Grandma Wu. "How is Ivanov doing? Does he know where the Americans are being held?"

"According to Ivanov, eight Americans were caught, and they're all in Bridge House," Grandma Wu reported sadly. "He drew a diagram of the layout of the prison cell they occupy. Their cell has a barred window that opens into the prison garden. We're trying to work out a rescue plan."

"In his letter, Ivanov also wrote that Major General Yonoshita, the commander of Bridge House, has promoted him to be his personal interpreter because of his language skills and good behavior," David volunteered. "Ivanov still works seven days a week but has been given permission to cook his own food. And Yonoshita allows him one visitor every two weeks."

"How lucky for Marat and Ivanov!" I said. "The two of them should do everything they can to stay friendly with Yonoshita. Perhaps they can persuade the major general to treat the Americans better."

"Ivanov *wants* to be Yonoshita's friend," Grandma Wu agreed, "but the friendship has to develop naturally so Yonoshita won't get suspicious."

I didn't normally take the lead, but I suddenly felt clear and confident about what needed to be done. Perhaps my months of training and my adventures in Nan Tian had made me strong.

"Marat told me once that Ivanov is a fabulous cook. He can turn the simplest vegetables into great-tasting dishes. Everyone likes to eat. I bet the food at Bridge House is pretty awful. Marat should take him lots of vegetables and herbs so Ivanov has something decent to cook with," I suggested. "If Ivanov starts cooking for Yonoshita, they'll gradually become friends."

"Good idea! You should develop a rescue plan around it," Grandma Wu said, looking at her watch. "You'd better be on your way home if your niang hasn't seen you yet. She's probably waiting for you."

"Yes. When you write to Big Aunt, will you tell her that from now on she can write to me directly at my father's address through the post office? No more pigeon mail. It will take forever, but it's better than nothing."

I was so happy about the escape of Lawson and his crew to Chungking that I ran all the way home in high spirits. I popped into the kitchen to say hello to Ah Yee first. The most delicious aroma greeted my nostrils from a pot of mushroom soup bubbling on the stove. Then I saw a colorful display of green peppers, purple eggplant and bright red tomatoes on the kitchen counter.

"Something smells wonderful! I've really missed your cooking, Ah Yee! I'm starving!"

"In spite of the war," Ah Yee said, "I still found all this in the market today. I'm making you a special dinner to celebrate your homecoming."

"Oh, Ah Yee. My mouth is watering already. Can I have a tiny piece of tomato? Yum! It's so sweet."

"What a shame I can't take you home to show you the village where I grew up." Ah Yee sighed. "You should see the size of my tomatoes. When I was your age, I'd climb up the bamboo lattices and pick the biggest and reddest tomato growing on the vine."

"Bamboo lattices?" I asked. "What for?"

"Don't you know anything, little city girl?" she teased. "The tomato plant is a vine. Vines need to be supported in order to grow, because their stems are so weak. In my village, we'd build lattices out of bamboo and suspend ropes between the poles for vines to grow on."

"What else grows on vines?" I asked eagerly. "Any other tasty vegetables?"

"Lots of vegetables grow on vines: string beans, sweet peas, bitter melons, cucumbers and squash to name a few. But now, Miss Ye Xian"—she lowered her voice to a whisper—"your niang wants to see you. Be careful! You'll find her in the living room listening to the radio."

As I walked gingerly toward the living room with my heart racing, I could hear a somber male voice reporting the news in Mandarin.

"This is a special announcement from the Kempeitei at Bridge House in Shanghai. According to our sister radio station JOAK in Japan, sixteen American bombers bombed four Japanese cities on April eighteenth. They indiscriminately destroyed schools and hospitals, killing and wounding civilians and a large number of schoolchildren. This inhuman attack on Japanese cultural and residential establishments has aroused

WIDESPREAD INDIGNATION AMONG THE JAPANESE PEOPLE.

"AFTER THE RAID, THE AMERICAN PLANES ESCAPED TO
CHINA. SOME OF THE AIRMEN PARACHUTED OUT AND LANDED
IN JAPANESE-OCCUPIED TERRITORY. ALTHOUGH MANY HAVE
BEEN CAPTURED, A FEW ARE STILL AT LARGE, INCLUDING FIVE
AIRMEN WHO CRASH-LANDED ON NAN TIAN ISLAND.

"IF ANYONE IS DISCOVERED HIDING AMERICAN FLIERS,
THEY WILL BE EXECUTED AND THEIR FAMILY SEVERELY
PUNISHED.

"WE ADVISE ALL CITIZENS TO BE VIGILANT AND TO
REPORT ANY KNOWLEDGE OF THE WHEREABOUTS OF THESE
AMERICAN CRIMINALS IMMEDIATELY TO THE JAPANESE
AUTHORITIES. A REWARD OF ONE MILLION CHINESE YUAN
WILL BE GIVEN TO ANYONE GIVING INFORMATION LEADING TO
THEIR CAPTURE. . . ."

Niang looked up and saw me standing fearfully at the door.
She turned off the radio and told me to come in.

She was perfectly coifed and sheathed in a bright green silk
Chinese dress. Diamonds sparkled on her hands, ears and wrist.
Her long fingernails were painted red, and the strong fragrance
of her expensive French perfume filled the air.

The memory of her sharp nails pressing against my throat
came back to me like a bad dream as I greeted her. I felt a wave
of nausea and longed to escape, but I dared not move. Ah Yee
came in with two cups of tea and gave me a sympathetic look.

"Sit down!" Niang commanded.

I sat at the edge of my seat and looked down at my feet.

"Where *were* you all these past weeks?" she asked.

"At Big Aunt's place," I lied.

"All the time you were gone?"

"Yes!"

"Did you go to school every day?"

"Almost every day."

"What did you do when you weren't at school?"

"Read books and listened to the radio."

"Was Big Aunt with you all the time?"

"Most of the time—"

"You're *lying!*" she screamed.

Her voice was so shrill that it made the hairs stand up on the back of my neck. More than that, it made me ache in some place that was buried deep within me. Mingled with my fear and my urgent wish to get away from her was a mysterious and inexplicable yearning: a chord of memory almost as ancient as life itself. I realized with a shock that in spite of everything, I still wished to please her. Yet, at the same time, I knew that she was evil.

Mercifully, at that moment, the phone rang.

Niang gave me a baleful look and picked it up. Immediately her tone turned sweet and courteous, entirely different from the one she had used while talking to me. In the middle of a long conversation about arranging a mah-jong game with the mayor's wife, she suddenly remembered that I was still waiting. With a wave of her hand, she dismissed me.

dysfunctional

179

CHAPTER 20

Running Away

 HINGS WENT BACK to the way they were before I met Grandma Wu. I tried to spend as much time away from home as possible. Niang was frequently away at her mah-jong games in the afternoons, so I spent a lot of time hanging around the bazaar. Every day after school I'd visit the bookstall and bury my nose in a *kung fu* novel. Grandma Wang, the new bookseller, was a professional artist and calligrapher. She tried to teach me the correct way of holding a brush, grinding ink sticks in water to make ink on ink stones, scripting Chinese characters and sketching trees and flowers. But my attempts at creating "art" failed miserably because I simply could not draw.

I dared not visit Grandma Wu at the academy, so I missed her and the boys terribly. Once or twice a week, Grandma Wu would make her way to the bookstall to see me. Depending on their schedules, one of the boys would sometimes join us. I was always hungry for news. It was a thrilling day when Marat told me he was now allowed to visit Ivanov every Sunday at Bridge House.

"I'm so glad you can visit him weekly now. How is he?" I asked. "What's it like in that prison?"

"Ivanov is amazing! Although he's dying to get out of jail, he never complains. As for Bridge House, it's more awful than you can ever imagine. Ivanov says the Japanese built it to provoke fear among the Chinese people."

"I'm sure Ivanov is right."

"I take fresh fruits and vegetables to Ivanov every week," Marat added. "My brother is cooking for Yonoshita pretty regularly now. They've become quite friendly. Sometimes they even eat together."

When he mentioned vegetables, I thought of what Ah Yee had told me, and a plan began to take shape in my mind.

"Make sure you take lots of string beans, tomatoes, sweet peas, bitter melons, cucumbers and squashes next week," I said. "Ask Ivanov to cook some tasty dishes with those vegetables."

"Why those in particular?"

"Because they are all vines. And vines can only grow if they are supported by lattices or ropes."

"So?"

"See if Ivanov can persuade Yonoshita to plant a vegetable garden in Bridge House," I suggested. "Maybe they'll put the prisoners to work, including the Americans. Then Yonoshita can have all the fresh vegetables his heart desires."

"But why are vines so important?" Marat was puzzled.

"It's not vines. It's the lattices and ropes supporting those vines, particularly if they're placed next to a wall. So convenient for anyone wanting to escape . . . ."

At home, I closeted myself in my room doing homework, reading novels and writing in my diary. Every evening before dinner, I would secretly practice my *kung fu* exercises behind closed doors. During mealtimes, I sat at my parents' table not saying a word, afraid that I might come up with the wrong remark. On weekends, I made a point of helping Ah Yee in the kitchen. I'd never forgotten the promise I made to myself to learn to cook, and I was determined to become as good a cook as the boys and Ah Yee.

By the middle of May, I was missing my aunt more than ever. Finally one day, Ah Yee said that a letter had come for me.

"I think it's from your aunt," she whispered. "Postmarked Nan Tian Island with no return address. It's definitely her handwriting. Is she visiting Nan Tian?"

I ignored her question. "Where's the letter?"

"Actually, it was more than a letter," Ah Yee said. "It was one of those cardboard packages used for sending books."

"Did she send me a book?" I asked, delighted at the prospect. "Give it to me!"

"Your stepmother has it," Ah Yee said.

"Why did you give it to *her*?" I asked, suddenly filled with premonition.

"I was following your father's instructions. He wanted all letters addressed to you to be given to them first."

"Even those from Big Aunt?"

"Especially those from Big Aunt. I don't think they believe your story about what you did during your absence from home. I heard your stepmother saying to your father yesterday that Big Aunt is a bad influence. If Niang has her way, she would prevent you from ever seeing your aunt again. She seems to hate her."

I kept thinking of Big Aunt's letter and could hardly concentrate on my homework or anything else. During dinner, my parents avoided looking at me. Although I was dying to ask, I was afraid of getting Ah Yee into trouble.

When dinner was almost over and we were peeling our fruit for dessert, Niang suddenly ordered Ah Yee to bring the package lying on her dressing table.

My heart leapt when I saw my aunt's familiar handwriting. Then I noticed with a sinking feeling that the package had already been opened.

"We have here a package sent to you by your aunt," Niang began with a smug smile. "It contains some *very* interesting material!"

"The package was addressed to me," I protested bravely. "May I ask who gave you the right to open it?"

Her smile vanished in an instant. "You are insolent and obnoxious! How *dare* you ask such a question? We opened it because your aunt is not to be trusted. She's a wicked woman who is out to destroy her family."

"I don't agree," I began. Seeing the sharp frown on my father's face, I quickly added, "But you are entitled to your own opinion, just as I am to mine."

She gave a cynical laugh. "I'm not about to argue with someone as stupid as you! See for yourself."

Trepidation rose quickly somewhere in my stomach as she handed me the package. I had a sudden foreboding of something dangerous lurking within, a mysterious object beyond my comprehension. Otherwise, why was Niang leering and capering as she dug her tentacles ever deeper into my heart? Worst of all, I had to cope with this situation alone, without help from anybody. Certainly not from my father.

What's in the package that can be so bad? I thought as I took it in my sweaty hand, trying to reassure myself. I looked up at Niang and glimpsed a chilling smile on her face. Was it *triumph* I saw written all over her features? What was she celebrating? Why was she so happy?

I had once seen a cat beside a pond, waiting to pounce on some hapless goldfish swimming in the water. I thought with something akin to horror, Niang is enjoying this! But why? Then I plunged my hand bravely into the package. Initially, my fingers felt nothing but a tangled nest of shredded paper padding. After groping around for a while, I finally pulled out a small, oblong cardboard box.

At first I was relieved, thinking I had worried over nothing. But then I opened the box. Inside was a pair of glittering silver flying wings, the same wings that the American pilot, Ted Lawson, had torn off his shirt and given to me on the night of his rescue. As I stared at the badge with my mouth half open in alarm, I heard Niang's cold voice saying, "What *is* this, and where did it come from?"

I pulled every scrap of shredded paper out of the package to look for Big Aunt's letter, but there was none.

"Didn't Big Aunt send a letter with this box? Where is it?" I asked.

"Answer me first!" she commanded.

"How would *I* know?" I said in a deliberately nonchalant voice. "What do *you* think it is?"

"You and your aunt are playing with fire!" she said menacingly. "Your father and I think this badge must have belonged to one of the American pilots. On the back of it are the words 'U.S. Army Air Corps.' If the Japanese find this in our possession, all of us will be given the death penalty!"

A shiver went down my spine. When I looked at Niang's cold, beautiful face, I felt a spasm of panic and fear. If I wasn't careful, something dreadful would happen.

"What does Big Aunt say in her letter?" I persisted desperately. "She sent it to *me*! It's *my* letter! Let me have it!"

"Your father tells me that your aunt's godmother lives in Nan Tian. He visited that island many times as a boy and has even been to Grandma Liu's house. He thinks your aunt must have been involved in some way with the Americans. Your aunt is a bad influence. In fact, she's downright dangerous! Your father and I have decided that you are to have nothing more to do with her."

A chasm opened and I could hardly breathe. I wanted to scream, but a voice in my head told me to remain silent. Then Father said sadly, "Big Aunt has always been patriotic, but this time she has gone too far. She must have helped the American airmen who crash-landed on Nan Tian Island."

"What's wrong with that?" I asked defiantly. "Whose side are you on, anyway? Japan, or China's ally, America?"

"How *dare* you speak to your father in that tone of voice!" Niang exclaimed. "You are getting more and more insolent! Without your parents, you are *nothing*! Do you hear me? *Nothing!*"

"I may be nothing," I replied, seething with rage, "but I want Big Aunt's letter. She sent it to *me*, not *you!*"

Without a word, Niang got up from the table and gave me a resounding slap on my right cheek. Then she slapped my left cheek with the back of her hand, as hard as she could.

"Get out of the room! From now on, you are not allowed to see your Big Aunt ever again. If you do, I will send you to an orphanage. Your problem is that you have bad blood from your dead mother. If you are smart, you will never mention a word to anyone about this emblem. Forget that you ever saw it. This goes for you too, Ah Yee!"

"What about Big Aunt?" I asked. "Are you going to tell the Japanese about her?"

"That's none of your business!" Niang said ominously. "As

far as you're concerned, your aunt has gone away and will never come back. Your father and I will decide what to do with this emblem. *And* with your aunt! Now get out!"

Ah Yee came into my room later that night and found me crying. She sat at the edge of my bed and burst into tears herself.

"I'm worried about what Niang might do to Big Aunt," I told her. "My stepmother is up to no good."

Ah Yee wiped the tears from my cheeks, bruised and swollen from Niang's slaps. "Miss Ye Xian! How did things reach *this* awful state between you and your niang? What will become of you?"

"Please help me!" I pleaded. "I must go to Nan Tian and rescue my aunt. I have friends who will help me. I have money. Remember the little red packages of money we children get from grown-ups during Chinese New Year? Father gave me a porcelain piggy bank a few years ago and told me to store all my money in it in case of an emergency. Well, *this* is the emergency!"

I rummaged through my drawers until I found my piggy bank. Without any hesitation, I broke it in half against the windowsill and emptied its contents on my bed. Ah Yee counted the money with me, and we were thrilled to find a total of forty-eight yuan and sixty fen.

"There is no going back now," I said. "Breaking my piggy bank was like breaking free from my parents. I'll leave the broken pieces on my desk, with a note telling them that I've gone to look for my aunt and not to worry about me. . . ."

"But you are still only a little girl of twelve," Ah Yee protested. "How do I know you'll be safe?"

"I know the food market where you shop every day. If I need you, I'll send someone there to contact you. I'll show them a photo to recognize you by. The person will say the code words: 'little green horse.' You must answer, 'old green horse.'"

"How did you come up with 'green horse' as a code?" Ah Yee asked.

"Easy! We were both born in the year of the horse! Green is my favorite color, and yours too. I trust you, Ah Yee. Don't look so worried. When I grow up, I'll take care of you. I promise."

"Just look after yourself and be very careful!" She sighed.

I packed a few of my most intimate possessions and stuck them in my schoolbag with my books. First of all, I took my black leather diary, and then my Imperial Yellow Growth Chart, toothbrush, pajamas, underwear and a group photo taken a long time ago when I was a baby. It showed my mama, my father, Big Aunt, Ah Yee and me having a picnic in the garden behind our house.

I slept very badly because I knew it was the last night I would spend in my father's house. Next morning, I ate breakfast at the usual time, took my schoolbag as if I was going to school and went to the Martial Arts Academy instead. The boys had already left, so I found Grandma Wu alone. One look at me and she told me I needed to sit down.

We sat opposite each other and I poured out my tale of woe. As my story progressed, she became increasingly alarmed.

"Do you know what your stepmother is planning to do with Lawson's flying wings?"

"Not exactly. I only know that she hates my aunt and plans to harm her."

"Is there any possibility that she might betray your aunt to the Japanese?"

I winced. "There's *every* possibility."

"Then your aunt's life is in danger. She must go to Chungking as soon as possible. Although the Japanese are angry at the Americans for invading their homeland, they resent us Chinese even more for helping them. Our agents have informed us that the Japanese high command in Tokyo is planning to do something dreadful to the people living on the coast of Zhejiang Province. They want to punish them so severely that nobody in China would ever dare help the Americans again."

"Is Big Aunt still in Nan Tian?" I asked, deeply afraid.

"I fear she's still looking after her godmother, Grandma Liu, in Nan Tian. I sent her a letter by pigeon immediately after your father took you back. I told her you missed her and that she should write directly to you at your father's address since you'd be living at home. In her return letter she mentioned that there were many more Japanese soldiers in Nan Tian. Since then, I haven't heard from her or my son."

"I wish I'd never asked for Big Aunt to write to me at my father's address. Oh, Grandma Wu! If only I could turn the clock back! I'm so worried. Will she be all right?"

"I don't know," Grandma Wu replied gravely. "These are troubled times. I'll send my son an urgent note by pigeon today. Maybe he'll be able to give us up-to-date information. For now, let's talk about you. What are your plans?"

I sprang out of my chair and knelt in front of her. "Please don't force me to go home! I beg you. My parents have forbidden me to see my aunt ever again. I would rather die than go home to my stepmother!"

"Calm down and sit in your chair. Let's analyze the situation. Since you have no intention of living with your niang ever again, you must go into hiding at once. Let's wait and see what your aunt wants you to do before deciding on anything else. She might even want to take you to Chungking with her.

"For the time being, you can stay here with me and the boys. Obviously, you can no longer go to school or show your face around the neighborhood. Never answer the phone and beware of every knock on the door. This is a matter of life and death, not only for you but for all of us.

"Instead of school, I want you to work out a rescue plan to get the American fliers out of Bridge House. Don't look so worried! Remember, the best cure for worry is to do something positive. Fearing the worst for your aunt is actually worse than the worst that can happen to her. That's because fear is endless and formless, whereas even the worst outcome has an ending."

I felt a surge of pride that Grandma Wu had faith in me to come up with an escape plan.

"What have you heard about the captured Americans?" I asked.

"Altogether, eight airmen were captured. We must never forget them! They have risked their lives for China. They are *en ren*—our benefactors. Five of the eight came from the plane *Bat Out of Hell*. Ivanov has provided Marat with their names: Bill Farrow, the pilot; Bobby Hite, the copilot; George Barr, the navigator; Jake DeShazer, the bombardier; and Harold Spatz, the engineer-gunner. Their plane ran out of fuel in Japanese-occupied territory, and all five parachuted into the waiting arms of Japanese soldiers.

"The other three fliers were from the *Green Hornet*, which ran dry less than four minutes from the coast. Their plane crashed into the sea and broke apart a short distance from shore. Two of the crew died in the crash. The three who survived were Dean Hallmark, the pilot; Robert Meder, the copilot; and Chase Nielsen, the navigator. Chinese guerrillas hid them at first, but they were betrayed and captured by the Japanese."

"How are they being treated?"

"Terribly! Ivanov tells us that all eight are now locked in a single cell crawling with lice, rats and bugs. They haven't been allowed to bathe, shave or change their clothes since their capture. They have to sit cross-legged on the floor, without talking or moving or even leaning their backs against the walls. Otherwise they get beaten. Food consists of maggoty rice and a few pieces of bread. Their cell is so small there isn't even enough floor space for everyone to lie down at the same time to sleep at night. They have to take turns. A naked lightbulb hangs from the ceiling and burns twenty-four hours a day. Their toilet is an open wooden bucket in one corner overflowing with excrement. Two of the airmen have already come down with dysentery and beriberi."

"We must get them out!"

"Their cell has a barred window twenty-five feet above the prison garden. The garden in turn is surrounded by a wall thirty feet high and faces a busy street."

"What are the bars made of?"

"Solid steel. Here's Ivanov's diagram of the layout of their cell. Study it carefully. We need you to come up with a plan!"

CHAPTER 21

Rescue Plans

STOPPED GOING TO school, went into hiding and helped Grandma Wu behind the closed doors of the Martial Arts Academy. I was told never to show my face at the window. The result was that I lived in a state of high anxiety, dreading the sound of any footsteps coming up the driveway and fearing every knock on the door. The worst part was not being able to leave the house to go outside, not even for a minute.

I showed David the photo of Ah Yee, and he was able to recognize her at the market on Saturday morning. She brought him ominous news. Niang had persuaded my father to file a missing person's report at the police station regarding my disappearance.

When I heard this, I was so scared that I begged Grandma Wu to let me cover all the windows in my bedroom. She gave me some scraps of fabric that the boys and I stitched crookedly together. Sam and I stood on David's and Marat's backs and tacked these blinds permanently to the windows, leaving my room in total darkness day and night.

Meanwhile, we were unable to establish contact with Big Aunt, Grandma Liu or anyone else at Nan Tian. Train services from Shanghai to both Chuchow and Linhai had been halted, and mail sent through the post office was returned marked "undeliverable." We sent numerous letters by pigeon but received no response.

On Sunday, Marat came back from Bridge House with reports from Ivanov.

"Ivanov says you must hurry if you want to rescue them," Marat told us. "They've been tortured and are in terrible shape. Because of bad hygiene and lack of food, all eight airmen are seriously ill. They're also going crazy, sitting cross-legged on the floor in their filthy cell with nothing to do day after day. Their faces, hands and legs are swollen and red from bug and rat bites. The pilot Dean Hallmark can't even stand. His copilot, Robert Meder, is semiconscious and close to death. Yesterday, Ivanov's overseer, Sergeant Sotojiro Tatsuta, ordered Hallmark, Farrow and Spatz to sign their names on blank sheets of paper. Later, the Kempeitei inserted false statements in Japanese above their signatures, claiming these were confessions made by the airmen. Since the statements had never been translated into English, the Americans had no idea what they'd signed."

Grandma Wu and I looked at each other in dismay. "This is terrible! You must hurry, CC, and come up with a plan for their rescue before they die out like flies!" She turned back to Marat.

"Is the news all bad?"

"No, I have good news too! Ivanov said that Yonoshita loves the vegetables and fruits I've been bringing every week. The string beans were such a big hit that Ivanov was finally able to persuade Yonoshita to start his own vegetable garden, with help from the prisoners!"

"How fantastic!" I beamed.

"Marat, please congratulate Ivanov on my behalf for getting gardening privileges for the airmen," Grandma Wu said. "For the time being, gardening will at least get the Americans out of their cells and give them a little sorely needed exercise."

For the next few days, with no school to go to, I sat under a small lamp in my darkened bedroom, scrutinizing Ivanov's diagram of the Americans' cell hour after hour. I felt a heavy sense of responsibility but was proud to be entrusted with this important task. Looking at a large map of Shanghai borrowed from the boys' school library, I saw that Bridge House was only half a mile away from the Bund (Embankment) and the Huang-pu River. The dangers were great, but after tussling with the problem for a long time, I finally figured out a plan that might work.

I asked Grandma Wu to call a special meeting.

The next evening, after dinner, we gathered in the same alcove where I had been initiated into the Dragon Society of Wandering Knights. I was touched to see that Grandma Wu had covered all the windows with floor-to-ceiling drapes. Instead of a candlelight ceremony held in semidarkness, Grandma Wu ordered us to close all the curtains and turn on the lights, one of which was focused on the scroll with the two large Chinese characters: *Fu Dao*, Tao of Buddha. A round table and five chairs were placed in the middle of the alcove. She then spread Ivanov's diagram and the map of Shanghai in front of us on the table.

"Lock all doors and ignore the doorbell while our meeting is in progress," she said. "Don't answer the telephone. We need to concentrate and vote on CC's plan this very evening."

Then she pointed to the *Fu Dao* scroll behind her head and said solemnly, "Every mission undertaken by members of our society will be carried out in strict accordance with the Tao of Buddha. We will never act out of vengeance or cruelty. Nor will we ever do anything against our conscience. CC, you may begin."

Everyone's eyes turned to me. My mouth felt dry, and my heart was pounding.

"My plan is based on Ivanov's diagram of Bridge House and his latest information," I began. "The American fliers are imprisoned in a single cell with steel bars on its window and door. Ivanov has developed an excellent relationship with the American prisoners, as well as with Major General Yonoshita. He has actually been able to persuade Yonoshita to plant a vegetable garden within the existing yard, using prison labor."

"Last Sunday I saw American and Chinese prisoners working in the garden," reported Marat, "digging and putting up lattice supports. They looked haggard and filthy. To prevent vendors seeing the prisoners' wretched condition, Yonoshita has given permission for gardening supplies to be dropped over the prison wall. And it looked as though the prisoners were working by themselves without supervision."

"Great! That's exactly what I was hoping for," I continued. "I propose that we hide hacksaw blades inside hollow bamboo tubes and throw them over the prison wall with the rest of the gardening supplies. I never forgot the story Sam told me of his friend Hans."

"He's the one who sawed through steel bars and escaped from the train to Auschwitz," said Sam.

"I think I can guess what you have in mind, CC." David smiled at me. "Ivanov should tell the Americans to use the blades to secretly saw through the steel bars of their cell window, right?"

I nodded and went on. "Lattices need ropes, and extra ropes could be hidden—"

I stopped at the sound of a key turning in the front door. Grandma Wu sprang up and rushed to the entrance hall with the rest of us closely behind. A weary figure with long hair and dusty clothes staggered in. It was Master Wu!

He was thin and exhausted. As Grandma Wu greeted him and they embraced each other, he burst into sobs.

"What is it, my son?"

"All is lost! All is lost!" he groaned incoherently.

At first, it was shocking to witness his tears. We looked at one another, unsure of what to do. Then I felt a sharp pain, somewhere below my neck, indicating something nameless and unbearable. I knew it would be dreadful, but I had to find out.

I ran forward and confronted my worst fear head-on. My whole world was falling apart, but I needed to hear the truth. I stood directly in front of Master Wu and asked, "Where is my aunt?"

He stared at me with tear-filled eyes and slowly shook his head. Then I said the terrible words that he could not bring himself to utter.

"She is dead, isn't she?"

This time he nodded.

For an instant, I could see nothing but darkness. My whole being was filled with a deep sense of loss. My beloved aunt was dead. That's all I knew. A surge of despair overwhelmed me. Big Aunt had been the center of my universe. Now there was no one. Everything was empty.

Grandma Wu put her arm around me and led me to a chair. I buried my face in her lap and sobbed like a baby, letting go of the anguish that flooded my heart. My desolation was profound, as if a part of me had been severed.

"Tell us what happened," she said to her son. "You'll feel better when you've unburdened yourself. Sharing your distress will lessen your sorrow."

Master Wu collapsed at our feet with a groan, and the three boys sat on the floor beside him.

"After you left, a squadron of Japanese soldiers came to Nan Tian looking for the American fliers," he said. "They salvaged part of the B-25 bomber that had crashed into the ocean and took it away to Japan for exhibitions around the country. Tokyo's leading newspaper, *Asahi Shimbun*, published photos of a torn metal wing and twisted landing gear tubing from the wrecked bomber to prove to the Japanese people that American planes had been destroyed.

"We thought everything would go back to normal after that. But a week later, there was a suspicious forest fire. The Japanese had probably set it deliberately to smoke out any possible American airmen who might still be hiding there. I went looking for Mei Mei, my panda, when the fire died down, and found her hiding on the top branch of a tall tree. She was alone. Her legs were charred, and she was very frightened."

"What did you do then?" David asked.

"Grandma Liu was still very ill, so I told Big Aunt to stay and look after her while I took my panda back to Sichuan Province. There I released her in the bamboo forests of Wulong, where she was born. I was away for a total of ten days."

He hesitated and his eyes filled again with tears.

"I should have suspected something was terribly wrong, because I couldn't get through by phone or buy a bus ticket from Sichuan to Yong Quan. On my way back by truck, foot and donkey, villagers along the coast on the mainland warned me to keep away from Nan Tian Island. Regular ferry crossings to the island had all been canceled. No boatman would take me.

"I finally hired a small sampan and sailed to Nan Tian alone at night. When I landed, a scene of unimaginable horror greeted my eyes. I saw bodies of men, women and children piled up and strewn about the beach. Blood everywhere. The place reeked of death and destruction. There were no other boats in the harbor. Grandma Liu's village had become an inferno. All the houses had been burned, and smoke was still rising from their charred and blackened foundations—"

"Big Aunt!" I interrupted in a hollow voice. "How did she die? Where did you find her?"

Master Wu ignored my questions. "As I was surveying the scene in horror and disbelief," he continued, "I heard someone calling my name. It was Li Cha."

"So Li Cha is still alive!" David exclaimed.

"Yes! He was one of the very few who survived. But he looked haggard and gaunt. Li Cha's father, Old Mr. Li, was the school principal and owned the hut on the beach that gave shelter to you and the Americans. Li Cha said that four days after I left, a whole division of Japanese troops arrived in gunboats seeking revenge. At first, they made an announcement in the village square for the people to surrender any hidden American fliers.

"When no one came forth, they became angry. The soldiers kicked doors open at random and terrorized the population. One or two of the fishermen must have squealed under torture because the soldiers headed straight for Old Mr. Li's house. There they found some of the gifts that Lawson and his crew had left behind for the children.

"They arrested the old man, wrapped him in a blanket, doused it with kerosene and ordered Li Cha's mother to set it aflame. When she refused, they bayoneted her and threw her body into a well.

"Li Cha had gone to warn Grandma Liu and Big Aunt. But there was no way Grandma Liu could run away. Big Aunt refused to leave without Grandma Liu, telling Li Cha that she was honor-bound to stay with her *gan ma ma*. Both Li Cha and Grandma Liu begged her but to no avail. They heard the footsteps and voices of the Japanese soldiers approaching. Li Cha hurried out the back door at the last minute, threw himself into a dry ditch and crawled away."

"What about Big Aunt?" I asked again.

"Li Cha only knows that she and Grandma Liu are both dead, but not how. The Japanese ordered everyone who had helped the Americans to assemble themselves in a straight line on the beach. Some of the fishermen who had carried the fliers did so and were immediately mowed down by machine-gun fire. The soldiers then went from house to house, shooting and bayoneting everyone in sight for two days. On the morning of their departure, they set fire to the entire village. The flames spread from building to building until they burned themselves out a few days later.

"Li Cha escaped only because he knew a cave where he used to hide as a boy. He said that the sky over Nan Tian was filled with so much black smoke that he could not see the sun during the day. He could smell the horrifying odor of burning flesh and hear the sound of the fire even from his cave, sizzling and crackling like a rushing wind from hell. When the Japanese finally departed, there were very few people still alive, only those who had secret hiding places. Most of the residents had either been killed directly or died in the fire."

"Why did this have to happen to Big Aunt?" I asked in anguish. "She was such a wonderful person. Why did she have to die? It's not fair."

There was a long silence. Then Sam came to my side. "My dad taught me a prayer once, when our Jewish relatives were being taken away from us one by one in Berlin. Would you like to hear it?"

I found it hard to speak, so I just nodded.

"It's from a book called Ecclesiasticus. Dad told me to learn it by heart, because reciting the words would bring me comfort wherever I might be. Perhaps you should learn it, too. It goes like this:

> *"When you gaze upon the dead, remember this:*
> *You have been shown more than you can understand.*
>
> *"Search not for what has been hidden from you.*
> *Seek not to comprehend what is so difficult to bear.*
> *Be not preoccupied with what is beyond your ken.*
>
> *"Mourn the dead, yes. Hide not your grief.*
> *Restrain not your sorrow or your lamentations.*
> *But remember: Suffering without end is worse than death.*
>
> *"Fear not death, for we are all destined to die.*
> *Fear not death, for we share it with all who ever*

lived and with all who ever will be.

"The dead are at rest. Let the pangs of memory rest too.

"As a drop of water in the immensity of the sea, as a grain of sand on the measureless shore, so are man's few days in the light of eternity.

"O God, our Father, You redeem our soul from the grave. Forsake us not in the days of our distress and desolation. Help us to live on, for we have placed all our hope in Thee."

CHAPTER 22

Last Letters

COULDN'T SLEEP THAT NIGHT. With all my heart, I yearned for just one more day with Big Aunt. I buried my face in my pillow and sobbed deep into the night, then tossed and turned until dawn. I must have dozed off eventually, because I woke to the sound of the front door banging shut. My room was in its usual state of perpetual darkness, so I had no idea what time it was.

Without turning on the light, I groped my way to the kitchen. There I found Grandma Wu. She was reading the back of a poster in the bright sunlight flooding through the window.

"The boys have gone to school, and Master Wu just left to look after some business matters," she said. "I thought I'd let you sleep."

"Is that another one of Ivanov's secret letters?"

"This is the first one we've received since Marat has been visiting him in prison. There have been unfortunate developments in Bridge House. We must deal with these issues when everyone is home this evening. Meanwhile, I need to talk to you about your future."

"My future?"

"Yes. I'm afraid the police are circulating posters, featuring your name and photo, around Shanghai. Next to your picture are the words 'Have you seen this girl?' followed by a telephone number. There's a hefty reward for turning you in. People will be looking for you everywhere."

"Please don't send me back!" I pleaded desperately. "I'd rather die! Besides, my parents *hate* me! I don't understand. Why do they want me back when they kicked me out in the first place?"

"Your father doesn't hate you. He loves you, but you're not his first priority. As for your niang, she simply wants to control you."

"But I'm happy living here with you! I've made friends with the boys. We're helping to fight the war. . . ."

"The happier you are away from your niang, the unhappier she will be. Misery loves company. She's an unhappy woman who wants you to grovel at her feet."

"It's too late! I hate her! She betrayed Big Aunt to the Japanese. She is a murderess! She is responsible for the death of my aunt."

"You have no evidence that your stepmother betrayed your Big Aunt. Besides, hate is destructive to your *Qi*! To lead a worthy life, you have to channel your *Qi* into positive goals!"

"How can I?" I complained. "I can't even think a single positive thought right now. My only goal is to avenge my aunt's murder."

"Revenge is not worthy of you. If you concentrate on revenge, you will keep those wounds fresh that would otherwise have healed. Instead of revenge, you should focus your energy on positive things, such as studying hard and becoming educated, reading widely and developing your mind, making friends and helping others—especially helping our American allies in Bridge House."

"How can I do all that when I can't even go to school? I wish my parents would leave me alone!"

"The question is," Grandma Wu said thoughtfully, "what can we do so that they will leave you alone?""

"The only way is to convince them that I'm already dead," I answered. "How many people do you think the Japanese killed in Nan Tian Island?"

"No one knows for sure. Thousands and thousands were massacred. My son has shown me some awful photographs. Our agents in Harbin have also discovered that the notorious Unit 731 of the Japanese army has dropped fleas infected with bubonic plague by aircraft over Nan Tian and the rest of Zhejiang Province. The Japanese are testing their biological weapons on us as punishment for helping the Americans."

"That's outrageous!" I cried. "Oh, Grandma Wu! How can they do this? Are they going to get away with their cruelty?"

"Of course not. The Japanese themselves must know in their

hearts that they're wrong to kill innocent civilians. I firmly believe that right makes might. So, let your conviction fill you with righteous *Qi* to go on resisting the enemy."

"You're right." I nodded as an idea came to me. "Those photos that Master Wu took of the massacre in Nan Tian should be kept somewhere safe. How about asking David to go to the market on Saturday and show them to Ah Yee? Tell her that I went to Nan Tian to look for Big Aunt. Unfortunately, the Japanese arrived soon afterward and killed everyone on the island—"

"—including Big Aunt and yourself!" Grandma Wu finished.

"Yes! My father will be shocked and saddened, but I don't think he will go to the Japanese. I believe he loves Big Aunt and me, even though he's under Niang's spell. When he sees the photographs, he'll know what the Japanese have done to his own people. After the war is over and I'm grown up, I'll come home and surprise him. By then, he'll be old and will need someone to look after him."

"This is a serious matter with many consequences," Grandma Wu said. "Let me think it over."

That evening, Grandma Wu asked Marat to read Ivanov's latest letter aloud:

"Horrific things have happened since Marat's last visit. You must hurry if you still plan to rescue them.

"A 'trial' was held in Bridge House. It was laughable because it was held in Japanese but no interpreter was provided for the Americans. The fliers were found guilty on the evidence of their false 'confessions.' Three of them were sentenced to death. The other five were given life imprisonment.

"The prison warden, Sergeant Sotojiro Tatsuta, ordered the three condemned airmen to write farewell letters to their families. I had to translate them into Japanese for the sergeant. We should keep a record of the last words of the three who died. Let their names live on forever. I had the honor of meeting all of them.

"First Lieutenant Dean Hallmark was twenty-eight years old and the pilot of the Green Hornet. He was born in Texas, and his nickname was Jungle Jim because of his splendid physique. He was tortured in Bridge House and lost more than sixty pounds. This was what he wrote in his last letter, to his father, mother and sister in Dallas, Texas:

'I hardly know what to say. They have just told me that I am liable to execution. I can hardly believe it. . . . I am a prisoner of war and thought I would be taken care of until the end of the war. . . . I did everything that the Japanese have asked me to do and tried to cooperate with them because I knew that my part in the war was over. I wanted to be a commercial pilot and would have *been if it hadn't been for this war. Mom, please try to stand up under this and pray.'*

"First Lieutenant Bill Farrow was twenty-four and the pilot of Bat Out of Hell. He wrote to his fiancée in South Carolina:

'Thank you for bringing to my life a deep, rich love for a fine girl. . . . You are, to me, the only girl that would have meant the completion of my life. Please write and comfort my mother, because she will need you—she loves you, and thinks you are a fine girl. . . .'

"To his mother he wrote:

'My faith in God is complete, so I am unafraid.'

"Sergeant Harold Spatz was twenty-one and the engineer-gunner of Bat out of Hell. He actually had his twenty-first birthday in Bridge House. He addressed his last letter to his widower father in Lebo, Kansas:

'I have nothing to leave you but my clothes, Dad. If I have inherited anything since I came of age, I wish you to have it also. And, Dad, I want you to know that I love you and may God bless you.

P.S. Just want to tell you that I died fighting for my country like a soldier.'"

We were all stunned when Marat finished reading. Tears ran down his face as he turned to Grandma Wu.

"We must speed things up!" His voice choked. "Otherwise they'll all be killed. Perhaps even Ivanov."

"What about your plan, CC?" David asked urgently.

I took a deep breath. "It's ready!" I said. "I've written it down to show everyone. The plan consists of eleven steps. I began plotting the airmen's escape on the day after we came back from Nan Tian. That was when Grandma Wu first told me they were being imprisoned in Bridge House. Because of this, the first three steps of my plan have already been implemented. Let me read it out loud.

"1. Coordinate everything with Ivanov. Tell him he has to escape with the Americans.

"2. Ivanov should gain Yonoshita's friendship and convince him to build a vegetable garden in Bridge House using prison labor.

"3. Building supplies should be moved directly from trucks parked on the street outside Bridge House and tossed over the wall into the garden.

"4. Hide hacksaws in hollow bamboo tubes that have been specially marked. Toss them with the rest of the bamboo into the garden.

"5. Build bamboo lattices close to the wall and plant vine-growing vegetables such as sweet peas, tomatoes, bitter melons, squash and string beans.

"6. Suspend long, sturdy ropes between bamboo poles to provide additional support for the vines. Ropes are needed for *the pilots*

airmen to lower themselves from their cell to the garden as well as from the garden wall to the street outside Bridge House.

"7. Best day to pick for the airmen's escape is the day of the Dragon Boat Festival. Best time is in the evening at ten-fifteen P.M. The guards will be celebrating the holiday and drinking at that time.

pilots

"8. Have false German identity papers for the fliers in case they are stopped by Japanese guards after their escape. Japanese and Germans are allies, but the guards may find it difficult to differentiate a German from an American.

"9. Provide armbands with the letter G, to go around the airmen's sleeves, and have German clothes in dark material made for the fliers. We have their approximate height and weight from Ivanov.

"10. Should we get separated from one another while rescuing the Americans from Bridge House, we will each make our own way to a safe house at 2105 North Szechuan Road, which has been rented by a member of the resistance. Grandma Wu tells me that this unique building happens to be situated in both the International Settlement (north half) and the French Concession (south half). The Japanese will need permission from the local French Consulate to search the premises. This delay will give us extra time if we need to make a quick getaway.

"11. Provide transportation for Americans from Bridge House to the safe house. Americans will change out of prison clothes there. Arrange for taxis to drive Americans from safe house to the Bund and board sampan. Then sail from Shanghai to Chungking via Huang-pu River and Yangtze River. Alert guerrillas along the way."

There was a short silence. "Any comments or suggestions?" I asked.

"Ivanov told me last Sunday that the Americans have tested their weight against the bamboo lattices they're erecting and think they'll be able to use them to climb over the prison wall. They also plan to hide some ropes to lower themselves from their cell into the garden," Marat reported.

"I'll hire a moving van on the night of the Dragon Boat Festival," Master Wu added thoughtfully. "I can park it outside the vegetable garden of Bridge House, at the spot normally occupied by the gardening supply truck. Once we're in the safe house, the Americans can have a wash and change from their prison uniforms into German outfits that my mother will make for them. We'll transfer the airmen into a large junk. Good plan, CC. Congratulations."

"Well done, CC!" Grandma Wu concluded. "The Dragon Boat Festival is only nine days away. We must start getting ready immediately. I've decided that we'll all escort the Americans to Chungking. Meanwhile, CC, you must remain in hiding."

Their words were music to my ears! What a sweet moment! Now I knew that I had well and truly earned my place in the Dragon Society of Wandering Knights. We were about to face our biggest challenge, together.

CHAPTER 23

The Future Belongs to Us

HE DAY OF THE DRAGON Boat Festival began with a heavy downpour at dawn. At first, we thought the acrobatic show scheduled for that afternoon at Du Mei Gardens would be canceled. Thunder roared, lightning flashed and rain came down in sheets.

After lunch, the weather gradually cleared. The boys dressed in their colorful satin costumes. Grandma Wu and I stayed behind to prepare for the Grand Escape. We burned all incriminating documents and buried our radio equipment in a lead-lined compartment hollowed out beneath a wall.

As I ironed the outfits Grandma Wu had sewn, I noticed that she had stitched stripes to the sleeves and added piping around the collars.

"You've made these jackets look like officers' uniforms!"

"That's right," Grandma Wu answered proudly. "When the

Americans put on these clothes, everyone will think they're officers from the German army. I've noticed that Japanese soldiers are particularly respectful of foreigners dressed in uniforms. Any uniform will do. Even a Boy Scout's! Just to be safe, however, I had German identity papers prepared for the airmen as well."

Master Wu and the boys came in to say they were leaving for the park. We wished one another good luck and arranged to meet outside Bridge House at 10:10 P.M. that evening. As they opened the door to leave, a beam of sunlight shafted in.

"Look at that cloud formation in the sky!" said Sam. "Doesn't it look just like a dragon?"

I peeked between the slats of the rattan shutters and saw a dragon-shaped, black-and-white cloud outlined clearly against a bright blue sky. A brilliant rainbow in red, orange, yellow, green, blue, indigo and violet arched out of the dragon's mouth.

"The dragon!" Master Wu exclaimed. "Symbol of the Society of Wandering Knights! It can soar up and fly into the sun, or dive down and touch the bottom of the ocean. It can wander at will to visit every corner of the universe or remain hidden among the waves. What a good omen that a dragon should appear in the sky at this moment. On the very day of the Dragon Boat Festival, no less!"

After the boys left, Grandma Wu and I made one hundred steamed *bao* (buns filled with cabbage and minced pork) for our forthcoming journey. We dressed in our peasant clothes and packed the buns and our belongings in backpacks. By 10 P.M. we were ensconced in a large moving van on the street outside

Bridge House, with Grandma Wu at the wheel and me hidden inside.

My heart raced as the hands of my watch approached 10:15 P.M. I pressed my body flat against the back panel of the van and felt my tongue sticking to the roof of my mouth. I could see through a small rear window. The surrounding streets were still packed with revelers enjoying the remaining hours of the Dragon Boat Festival. At 10:10 P.M., Master Wu and the boys positioned themselves at street corners, mingling with the crowd.

At precisely 10:15 P.M., four emaciated men dressed in prison clothing clambered awkwardly over the rear wall of Bridge House and slid down a rope, one after another. A murmur went through the throng, followed by a hush. Everyone stared. It gradually dawned on people that these were inmates breaking out of jail. I wanted to scream out words of encouragement to the airmen, but knew I mustn't!

To my surprise, nobody tried to halt their flight. Instead, everyone seemed to be on the side of the escapees. Some onlookers even stretched out their arms to offer a helping hand. Master Wu suddenly stepped forward and I heard him say, "Ivanov!" A fifth man poked his head above the wall and scrambled down. He led the prisoners quickly to our van. Grandma Wu had the engine running. Exhaust fumes billowed out from the tailpipes. The crowd dispersed as if on cue, leaving the road clear for us to make a quick getaway.

At that moment, I heard the sound of boots pounding the

pavement behind us. Someone called out, "Japanese patrolman!" All at once, David took a sling out of his pocket and catapulted a pebble into the air. It shattered the solitary street lamp and plunged the street into darkness. As our van pulled away, our headlights caught Marat and Sam raising a length of wire they had tied to two trees. The lone Japanese pursuer tripped and sprawled onto the ground. No one moved to help him back onto his feet.

David sprinted forward and hurled himself at the patrolman, who launched a flying kick at David's head. Quick as a dragon striking, David caught the soldier's ankle and twisted it. Propelled by his own momentum, the man lost his balance and fell heavily a second time. As he lay there stunned, with all the breath knocked from his body, the boys scattered in different directions and vanished into the crowd. They would take different shortcuts and make their own way to the safe house.

Inside the van, Ivanov introduced us to Chase Nielsen, Jake DeShazer, George Barr and Bobby Hite. Robert Meder, the copilot of the *Green Hornet*, was so sick that he'd been unable to escape with the others.

Ivanov and the airmen struggled into the uniforms we'd brought for them as we sped through the empty late-night streets to North Szechuan Road. Everything went according to plan. Master Wu unlocked the back gate, and Grandma Wu parked inside the garage. The men had a quick wash and a rough shave in the bathroom of the empty house. The three boys soon joined us. It was touching to see Marat and Ivanov together. They embraced and helped us burn the prisoners' uniforms in the living room fireplace.

Although pitifully thin, Ivanov and the four airmen looked impressive in their new German officers' uniforms. We got into taxis, driven by our agents, for the short ride to the Bund. No one challenged us or gave us a second glance as we boarded two sampans. We were ferried directly onto a large junk anchored in the middle of the Huang-pu River, weaving between the many colorful boats that had taken part in the Dragon Boat Race earlier. Their bows were painted in brilliant colors, and flags flew from the tops of their masts.

Inside the main cabin of the junk, Grandma Wu served the *bao* we had brought, while Master Wu brewed tea. There was a breeze, and the junk traveled steadily westward toward Chungking. By the light of a small oil lamp, I took my first proper look at the prisoners. I was horrified to see how ill they really were. They seemed overwhelmed by everything that had happened to them.

One of them asked me, "What's your name, little girl?"

"My Chinese name is Ye Xian, but my English name is CC," I answered shyly.

"I'm Jacob DeShazer, but my friends call me Jake," he said. I saw that his arms and hands were covered with angry boils. "On behalf of the five of us, I want to thank all of you from the bottom of our hearts for risking your lives to rescue us."

217

"It's nothing," I said. "I hate the Japanese. They killed my aunt."

He looked at me for a long time before he spoke again. "I did plenty of thinking in that prison. The Japanese, they sure haven't treated us decently. They tortured and starved us, and even executed three of us on trumped-up charges." He shut his eyes for a moment.

"My body's wrecked," he continued. "I could spend the rest of my life hating the Japanese. But hate is not erased by hate. There's no doubt in my mind that Japan will lose this war. Should I spend the rest of my life pursuing revenge? Or should I try to do something bigger, something that will live on even after I'm gone? The only way of turning the tables on those who did us wrong is to do them good.

"Your life is just beginning. Take my advice; don't live out of hatred. It won't make your life meaningful."

"What are you going to do now that you're free?" I asked. "Will you go back to America and start a business?"

"No way," Jake said. "These last few months, I've been wondering what will happen to the Japanese after they lose the war. They're so convinced that they'll win; it's going to be a big blow to them when they lose. But what if they should discover Jesus and the power of forgiveness through losing the war? In that case, their military defeat would turn out to be their greatest victory.

"When the war is over, I'm going to train as a missionary. I'll go to Japan, if I can, and teach the Gospel among the Japanese people. I hope to bring them peace."

Everyone was silent for a long time as we mulled over his words. Then Marat said, "My brother, Ivanov, and I are Muslims. Sam is Jewish. David is a Christian like you. Grandma Wu is a Buddhist, and CC doesn't know what she wants to be yet. Your intentions may be good, but what if the Japanese people are happy with their own beliefs?"

"That's a good question," Jake replied.

"Isn't religion an accident of fate?" Marat persisted. "Ivanov and I are Muslims because our mother was a Muslim. Sam's parents were Jewish, and David's parents were Christians. Grandma Wu's parents were probably Buddhist—"

"Religion is, indeed, an accident of fate," interrupted Master Wu. "It's my opinion that when we adopt the belief that our lives are ruled by a higher authority, we shouldn't limit that authority or give it a name. The ancient philosopher Lao Tzu wrote a book about this twenty-five hundred years ago, the Book of Tao.

"I believe it's wiser not to ask what this religion or that religion might be, or the name of this god or that god, but simply to think of Heaven, to cultivate a right attitude toward Heaven, without focusing on specific names.

"The essential beliefs of the major religions don't differ very much. The variations we notice are often the result of our own narrowness of vision.

"If you look at a bouquet of flowers and focus your gaze on a single red bloom, you won't see all the other blossoms. When your eye is not fixed on any one flower, and you face the bouquet with an open mind, then all the flowers become visible to you. But if a single flower alone holds your eye, it will be as if the remaining flowers are not there."

"Marat, Sam and I have had many arguments in the past because of our religious beliefs," said David. "Each of us thinks his religion is the best and only true religion."

"You three aren't alone!" Grandma Wu said. "Throughout history, there have been religious wars. Although I am a Buddhist, I agree with my son's concept of the Tao of Heaven. Unless all of us can accept that fundamentally there's no difference between the various major religions, our world will never be at peace."

"One can get to the same destination via many different paths," Master Wu said. "The Tao of Heaven is the source of our conscience. It manifests itself through kindness, morality and clarity of judgment. When people acquire the Tao of Heaven, it becomes part of their nature. They become virtuous and happy."

The boys looked at the airmen and then at one another. "Allah is great!" Marat finally conceded. "I never thought of it your way before, but I agree that we can reach Allah by taking different paths."

"Right!" agreed Sam. "The goal of all religions is the same. It is the realization that God is in our mind."

As our junk sailed briskly westward along the Yangtze River, I couldn't help but think of Big Aunt and my father. So much had happened since that first afternoon, when I watched the boys' acrobatic show and David had pulled his card out of my ear.

I left the cabin and stood at the bow of the junk, feeling sad and alone. I knew that Grandma Wu hadn't yet contacted Ah Yee or shown her the photos of the massacre at Nan Tian. Now that I was on my way to Chungking, there was no longer any need to tell Ah Yee or my father that I'd been murdered by the Japanese.

The ache for my family gripped me like a vice. It was devastating to think that I would never see Big Aunt again. My aunt was gone, but what should I do about my father? Would I ever see him again? Would he remember that he once had a daughter who adored him? What should I do? What should I do?

Our junk was pulling farther and farther away from the lights of Shanghai toward Chungking and freedom. Freedom! The word rang in my head over and over like sweet music. I thought of my last evening at home: how Father had allowed Niang to open my letter from Big Aunt without my permission; how he had remained silent throughout my inquisition; how he had not intervened, even when she slapped and berated me. It was as if he no longer had any will to voice his own opinion. Did it really matter to him whether I lived or died?

A voice behind me said, "What are you thinking?"

I turned and saw David, Sam and Marat. I wondered who had spoken. Then David said, "I know it's terrible to lose your Big Aunt, but remember, you will never be alone again. You are our *Xiao Mei*, little sister, a fellow member of the Dragon

Society of Wandering Knights. Besides, we need you for our future missions. This is just the beginning."

"I was wondering what to do about my father."

There was a short silence, then Sam said, "Maybe this will help you. It's from a book of Jewish writing called the Zohar: 'Honor your father and mother, even as you honor God, for all three were partners in your creation.'"

"Why don't you telephone your dad when you get to Chungking?" Marat said. "You'll be safe from the Japanese there. He must be worried about you. We hate to see you sad like this. Now that we are fellow members, your pain has become our pain as well."

I thought of phoning my father. But the image that came to mind was my meeting him at the front door of our house when Ah Yee brought me home from the academy. How awkward and tongue-tied we both were. There had been so much I wanted to say . . . but the mood and circumstances were all wrong. And in the end I had said nothing at all.

No. I needed to communicate with him in a different way. It should happen on an auspicious day of my choosing: a special day dedicated solely to telling him what I longed to express. I would wait for the right moment and place, and search for the necessary words to convey all that was buried within my heart. Hopefully, if I was very lucky, I'd be able to give him my truest explanation . . . and he would understand.

"Because of your friendship and advice," I said, "I now know what I must do. When we get to Chungking, I'm going to write my father a letter. In it, I'll tell him about Big Aunt's murder and everything I've been unable to say since Niang came into our lives. I'll also try to put in my heart and spirit. Perhaps such a letter will bring him consolation and solace . . . and me too, in the writing of it."

Sam nodded and took out from his pocket his piece of yellow silk. The four of us held hands and chanted in one voice,

*"We are in China at this moment in history for a reason.
We are here to make a difference. We are children of destiny
who will unite East and West and change the world. The
future belongs to us!"*

Historical Note

Chinese Cinderella and the Secret Dragon Society is a fantasy based on a true incident that took place in China during World War II. To understand the story's historical background, we need to go back to the first half of the nineteenth century.

My grandfather Ye Ye was born in Shanghai in the year 1878. He told me that his father, my great-grandfather, was born in 1842, the same year that China lost a war against Britain known as the Opium War. As a result of the peace treaty, five port cities along China's coast were placed under foreign rule. In treaty ports such as Shanghai in the 1940s, we Chinese lived as second-class citizens under the British, French, American, Japanese and other "conquerors."

The best areas of Shanghai were turned into foreign settlements (also called Concessions), which were governed by foreign consuls according to foreign law. Disputes were judged according to British law in the British Settlement (also named the International Settlement) and French law in the French Concession.

In 1911, when my Ye Ye was thirty-three years old, China underwent a revolution, and the imperial Manchu court in Beijing (Peking) was overthrown. Sun Yat-sen became president and proclaimed China a republic. After Sun's death in 1925,

General Chiang Kai-shek became China's leader.

Despite the change of government, China remained weak. Meanwhile, Japan was pursuing a policy of military expansion. In 1931, Japan invaded Manchuria in northeast China. Six years later, in July 1937, Japan declared war on China. For the next four years, Japan took control of China's coast but did not invade the foreign concessions. Chiang Kai-shek fled up the Yangtze River and moved his capital to Chungking, a city eight hundred miles west of Shanghai.

On December 7, 1941, Japan bombed Pearl Harbor in Honolulu and declared war on the U.S. and Great Britain. A few hours later, Japanese soldiers marched into Shanghai's International Settlement, eventually interning all British and American residents. Since France had fallen to Japan's ally Germany one year earlier and Shanghai's French Concession was under the administration of Vichy France, the Japanese did not intern the French.

To govern China's occupied territories, Japan set up a puppet regime headed by Wang Ching-wei. However, many of Wang's Chinese troops resented the Japanese and secretly sided either with Chiang Kai-shek or the Chinese Communists.

My father bought a house in the French Concession of Shanghai in 1942 and spent the next six years there. I went to a French convent school two miles from home and walked to and from school every day. Many of the scenes described in this book were culled from my memory.

On April 18, 1942, sixteen U.S. bombers under the command of Jimmy Doolittle took off from the aircraft carrier USS *Hornet* and bombed four Japanese cities. None was shot down. The *Ruptured Duck* and another plane crashed into the sea near the island of Nan Tian. All ten crew members survived the crash, but the pilot of the *Ruptured Duck*, Ted Lawson, had to have his leg amputated.

Other crewmen were not so lucky. Eight men from two other U.S. planes were captured by the Japanese after their planes crashed in Japanese-controlled territory.

After the raid, the Doolittle Raiders, as they were known, became famous throughout the world. For the first time in the history of Japan, the sacred motherland had been violated and bombed by the enemy. In their fury and humiliation, the Japanese unleashed a savage attack on the defenseless Chinese people for helping the airmen.

The bloodbath began on May 15, 1942, and went on for three months. To seek revenge, 148,000 Japanese troops were sent into Zhejiang Province. Countless numbers of Chinese were killed when Japanese planes dropped anthrax spores as well as fleas infected with bubonic plague on the hapless populace. Many who died had never even heard of the Doolittle Raid.

"When the Japanese finally withdrew in August 1942," the historian David Bergamini wrote in his book *Japan's Imperial Conspiracy*, "they had killed 250,000 Chinese, most of them civilians. The villages at which the American fliers had been entertained were reduced to cinder heaps, every man, woman and babe in them put to the sword. In the whole of Japan's eight-year war with China, the vengeance on Zhejiang province would go down unrivaled. . . ."

An outraged Chiang Kai-shek sent the following cable to the U.S. State Department in 1942: "After they had been caught unawares by the falling of American bombs on Tokyo, Japanese troops attacked the coastal areas of China where many of the American fliers had landed. These Japanese troops slaughtered every man, woman and child in these areas—let me repeat— these Japanese troops slaughtered every man, woman and child in these areas, reproducing on a wholesale scale the horrors which the world had seen at Lidice* but about which the people have been uninformed in these instances."

This book is a fantasy and describes the rescue of the crew of the *Ruptured Duck* from Nan Tian Island by four children who were members of a secret resistance society. The children also engineer a break-out of four captured U.S. airmen from Bridge House, an infamous Japanese prison and torture chamber. Although these children are characters from my imagination and never existed in real life, their backgrounds are historically accurate. Children of mixed race were called *za zhong* and were very much despised in Shanghai during the 1940s.

*On June 10, 1942, the Nazis destroyed the village of Lidice in Czechoslovakia after the Nazi official Reinhard Heydrich was assassinated there. They killed 172 men and boys and sent all the women and children to concentration camps, where most of them died.

The real names of the U.S. airmen were used in this book. However, in order to maintain the flow of the narrative, I took certain liberties with the time frame as well as the ages and the eventual fates of the captives.

In actuality, none of the U.S. crewmen escaped from prison. After their capture, they were first taken to Tokyo before being sent back to China and incarcerated in Bridge House. One died of malnutrition in prison and three were executed as described. The letters quoted in the chapter titled "Last Letters" are authentic and came from the pens of Dean Hallmark, Bill Farrow and Harold Spatz just before they died.

In August 1945, Japan lost the war and surrendered unconditionally to the allies. The four captured U.S. crewmen who survived their imprisonment were released. One of the four, Jake DeShazer, became a missionary and returned to Japan where he spent thirty years of his life (1948–1978).

You can learn more about the history of the USS *Hornet* by looking up the website www.uss-hornet.org or you can visit the Hornet Museum in Alameda, near San Francisco, California.

Chinese Cinderella and the Secret Dragon Society is my attempt on the part of one Chinese-American writer to inform the world of the horrors of war.

Glossary of Chinese Words

FAMILY, NAMES AND PLACES

Ah Sun 阿孫	a maid at CC's home
Ah Yee 阿姨	CC's wet nurse
Chiang Kai-shek 蔣介石	Chinese Nationalist leader
Da Ge 大哥	Big Brother
Da Ma 大馬	the homing pigeon
Da-wei 大慰	David
Er Ge 二哥	Second Older Brother
Fu Dao 佛道	Tao (Way) of Buddha
Gan ma ma 乾媽媽	godmother
Hui Men 海門	Sea Gate
Li Cha 李茶	Charlie
Linhai 臨海	City in Zhejiang province
Ling Ling 玲玲	David's dolphin
Liu Nai Nai 劉奶奶	Big Aunt's godmother; Grandma Wu's neighbor
Long Xia Hui 龍俠會	Dragon Society of Wandering Knights
Master CY Wu 吳師傅	Grandma Wu's son
Mei Mei 美妹	Master Wu's panda
Nan Tian Dao 南田島	Nan Tian Island
Niang 娘	Mother

Niu Zhou Shan 牛洲山	Cow Continent Mountain
San Ge 三哥	Third Older Brother
San Men Wan 三門灣	Three Doors Bay
Tai-ji tu 太極圖	Diagram of the Great Ultimate
Wu Nai Nai 吳奶奶	Grandma Wu
Wu Shu Xue Shiao 武術學校	Martial Arts Academy
Xiao Bao Bei 小寶貝	precious little treasure
Xiao Mei 小妹	Little Sister
Ye Jia-lin 葉家林	CC's father
Ye Jia-ming 葉家明	Big Aunt
Ye Xian 葉限	Chinese Cinderella (CC)
Ye Ye 爺爺	grandfather
Yi Jing 易經	Book of Changes
Yong Quan 湧泉	Gushing Spring

SAYINGS

Bai zhe bu nao. 百折不撓	Stick to your goal despite a hundred set-backs.
chu shen ru hua 出神入化	uncanny skill that is almost supernatural
Chu sui san hu, *wang Qin bi Chu.* 楚雖三戶亡秦必楚	Even if there are but three families left in Chu, the Qin empire will be toppled by a native son of Chu.
suo xiang wu di 所向無敵	irresistible force that is unconquerable
tong gan gong ku 同甘共苦	share bitter and sweet together
tong zhou gong ji 同舟共濟	stick together through thick and thin
Yin shui si yuan. 飲水思源	When drinking water, remember the source.
yu su bu da 欲速不達	more haste, less speed
Zi qiang bu xi. 自強不息	Motivate yourself to study hard and be strong always.

WORDS AND PHRASES

bao 包	buns filled with cabbage and minced pork
Chan 禪	zen/deep meditations
dyana 禪	meditation (see *Chan*)
en ren 恩人	benefactors
gu yi 故憶	the past
Gu Yi He 故憶盒	Memory Vision Box
Gua 卦	divine emblem
gun shui 滾水	rolling water (water that has been boiled)
jiang hu 江湖	rivers and lakes
Jiao 教	religion/to teach
kai shui 開水	opened water (water that has been boiled)
kung fu 工夫	(gong fu) mastery of a difficult task
mah-jong 麻將	game played with pieces called tiles
Ni hau? 你好	How are you?
Qi 氣	energy/life force
qi pao 旗袍	Chinese dress with Mandarin collar
shou zu 手足	hands and feet on the same body
Tao 道	Way
Tai chi quan 太極拳	martial art/meditative exercises/shadow-boxing

tong ren 同人	like-minded people
wei lei 未來	the future
Wei Lei He 未來盒	Future Vision Box
Wu 悟	mindful awareness
wu shu 武術	martial arts
Xiao 孝	respect for elders
yang 陽	male force that regulates the universe: male energy (positive, bright, warm)
yin 陰	female force that regulates the universe: female energy (negative, dark, cool)
you xia 游俠	wandering knights/historical heroes
yuan 元	Chinese dollar
yuan fen 緣分	predestined affinity
za zhong 雜種	mixed race, bastard, son of a bitch

The Chinese Zodiac

The Chinese zodiac is a fascinating part of Chinese culture. In chapter two, the author explains all about its origin and significance. To find out your animal sign, check the chart for the year you were born.

THE YEAR OF THE RAT
(1936, 1948, 1960, 1972, 1984, 1996, 2008)

You are imaginative, charming and generous. You have big ambitions, work hard to achieve your goals, and are a perfectionist. You tend to be quick-tempered and can be critical of others. You get along well with Dragons, Monkeys and Oxen.

THE YEAR OF THE OX
(1937, 1949, 1961, 1973, 1985, 1997, 2009)

You are a born leader and inspire confidence in others. You are methodical and skilled with your hands. You are usually easy-going, but you can be stubborn and hot-tempered. You are most compatible with Snakes, Roosters and Rats.

THE YEAR OF THE TIGER
(1938, 1950, 1962, 1974, 1986, 1998, 2010)

You are sensitive, emotional and loving; carefree and courageous. You can be short-tempered and often come into conflict with authority figures. You are a deep thinker; you can't make up your mind and yet you make hasty decisions. You get along well with Horses, Dragons and Dogs.

The Year of the Rabbit
(1939, 1951, 1963, 1975, 1987, 1999, 2011)

You are talented and affectionate, admired and trusted by others. Although you like to gossip, you are tactful and kind. You are wise and even-tempered, and usually don't take risks. You are compatible with Goats, Pigs and Dogs.

The Year of the Dragon
(1940, 1952, 1964, 1976, 1988, 2000, 2012)

You are energetic, popular and fun-loving. You are also honest, sensitive and brave. You appear stubborn, but you are really soft-hearted and sensitive. You are compatible with Rats, Snakes, Monkeys and Roosters.

The Year of the Snake
(1941, 1953, 1965, 1977, 1989, 2001, 2013)

You are a deep thinker and very wise. You are sympathetic and try to help those who are less fortunate, but sometimes you can be quite selfish. Although you appear calm, you are intense and determined. You are most compatible with Oxen and Roosters.

THE YEAR OF THE HORSE
(1942, 1954, 1966, 1978, 1990, 2002, 2014)

You are popular, quick-witted and adventurous. You are hard-working and very independent. You are wise and perceptive, but can be impatient and selfish. You get along with Tigers, Dogs and Goats.

THE YEAR OF THE GOAT
(1943, 1955, 1967, 1979, 1991, 2003, 2015)

You are creative, artistic and warm-hearted. You are also gentle, compassionate, and timid by nature. You strongly believe in your convictions, but you can be pessimistic. You are compatible with Rabbits, Pigs and Horses.

THE YEAR OF THE MONKEY
(1944, 1956, 1968, 1980, 1992, 2004, 2016)

You are clever, skillful and lots of fun. You are well-liked and you make friends easily, but you sometimes can't be trusted. You are strong-willed and good at making decisions. If you can't do things right away, you get depressed quickly. Monkeys get along with Dragons and Rats.

The Year of the Rooster
(1945, 1957, 1969, 1981, 1993, 2005, 2017)

You are hard-working, capable and talented. You are skilled at what you do, and you like to keep busy. You are good at making decisions. You are a little eccentric, outspoken and sometimes selfish. Roosters are compatible with Oxen, Snakes and Dragons.

The Year of the Dog
(1946, 1958, 1970, 1982, 1994, 2006, 2018)

You were born to succeed. You are loyal, honest and intelligent and inspire confidence in others. You can be sharp-tongued and stubborn, and tend to worry too much. You are compatible with Horses, Tigers and Rabbits.

The Year of the Pig
(1947, 1959, 1971, 1983, 1995, 2007, 2019)

You are honest, reliable, and extremely loyal. You are kind to those you love and you are a good companion. Although you are hot-tempered, you don't like to argue. You are goal-oriented, but can be impulsive. Pigs will get along with Rabbits and Goats.

Bibliography

Bergamini, David. *Japan's Imperial Conspiracy.* New York: William Morrow, 1971.

Map of Shanghai, 1940: Collar, Hugh. *Captive in Shanghai.* Hong Kong: Oxford University Press, 1990.

Letters from Bill Farrow, Harold Spatz, and Dean Hallmark: Glines, Carroll V. *Four Came Home: The Gripping Story of the Survivors of Jimmy Doolittle's Two Lost Crews.* Princeton, N.J.: D. Van Nostrand, 1966.

International Military Tribunal, Far East, National Archives, RG 331.

Lawson, T. W. *Thirty Seconds Over Tokyo.* New York: Random House, 1943.

Excerpt from the book of Ecclesiasticus from: Rosten, Leo. *Infinite Riches: Gems from a Lifetime of Reading.* New York: McGraw-Hill, 1979.

Schultz, Duane. *The Doolittle Raid.* New York: St. Martin's Press, 1988.

Shanghai. New York:

oolittle Raider Who Turned
ight and Life Press, 1950.